SOUTH OF THE BORDER, WEST OF THE SUN

Haruki Murakami was born in Kyoto in 1949. He met his wife, Yoko, at university and they opened a jazz club in Tokyo called *Peter Cat*. The massive success of his novel *Norwegian Wood* (1987) made him a national celebrity. He fled Japan and did not return until 1995. His other books include *after the quake*, *Dance Dance Dance*, *Hard-boiled Wonderland and the End of the World*, *A Wild Sheep Chase*, *The Wind-up Bird Chronicle*, *Kafka on the Shore*, *After Dark*, *Underground*, his first work of non-fiction, and *Sputnik Sweetheart*. He has translated into Japanese the work of F. Scott Fitzgerald, Truman Capote, John Irving and Raymond Carver

Philip Gabriel is associate professor of Japanese literature at the University of Arizona. He has translated Haruki Murakami's *Sputnik Sweetheart* and *Underground* (with Alfred Birnbaum), as well as the work of Senji Kuroi and Masahiko Shimada. He is the co-editor of an anthology of essays, *Oe and Beyond: Fiction in Contemporary Japan*.

Haruki Murakami

SOUTH OF THE BORDER, WEST OF THE SUN

TRANSLATED FROM THE JAPANESE BY
Philip Gabriel

VINTAGE BOOKS
London

This translation is dedicated to Mika-P.G.

Published by Vintage 2003

11 13 15 17 19 20 18 16 14 12

Copyright © Haruki Murakami 1992
English translation © Haruki Murakami 1998

Haruki Murakami has asserted his right under the Copyright, Designs and Patents Act 1988 to be identified as the author of this work

First published in 1992 with the title
Kokkyō no minami, taiyō no nishi by
Kodansha Ltd, Tokyo

First published in Great Britain in 1999 by
The Harvill Press

Vintage
Random House, 20 Vauxhall Bridge Road,
London SW1V 2SA

www.vintage-books.co.uk

Addresses for companies within The Random House Group Limited can be found at: www.randomhouse.co.uk/offices.htm

The Random House Group Limited Reg. No. 954009

A CIP catalogue record for this book
is available from the British Library

ISBN 9780099448570

The Random House Group Limited supports The Forest Stewardship Council (FSC), the leading international forest certification organisation. All our titles that are printed on Greenpeace approved FSC certified paper carry the FSC logo. Our paper procurement policy can be found at
www.rbooks.co.uk/environment.

Printed in the UK by CPI Bookmarque, Croydon, CR0 4TD

1

My birthday is January 4, 1951. The first week of the first month of the first year of the second half of the twentieth century. Something to commemorate, I suppose, which is why my parents named me Hajime – "Beginning", in Japanese. Other than that, a 100 per cent average birth. My father worked in a large stockbroker's, my mother was a typical housewife. In the war, my father was called up as a student and sent to fight in Singapore; after the surrender he spent some time in a POW camp. My mother's house was burned down in a B-29 raid in 1945. Their generation suffered most from the long war.

When I was born, though, you'd never have known there'd been a war. No more burned-out ruins, no more army of occupation. We lived in a small, quiet town, in a house which my father's company provided. The house was pre-war, somewhat old but roomy enough. Pine trees grew in the garden and we even had a small pond and some stone lanterns.

The town where I lived was typical middle-class suburbia. My school friends all lived in neat little terraced houses; some might have been a bit larger than mine, but you could count on them all having similar entrances and pine trees in the garden. The works. My friends' fathers were employed in companies or else they were professionals of some sort. Hardly anyone's mother worked. And almost everyone had a cat or a dog. No one I knew lived in a flat or an apartment. Later on I moved to another part of town, but it was nearly identical. The upshot of this is that until I moved to Tokyo to go to college, I was convinced everyone in the whole world lived in a single-family home with a garden and a pet, and commuted to work in a suit. I couldn't imagine a different lifestyle.

In the world I grew up in, a typical family had two or three children. My childhood friends were all members of such stereotypical families. If not two kids in the family, then three; if not three, then two. Families with six or seven kids were few and far between, but even more unusual were families with only one child.

I happened to be one of the unusual ones, since I was an only child. I had an inferiority complex about it, as if there was something different about me, that what other people all had and took for granted I lacked.

I detested the term *only child*. Every time I heard it, I felt I was missing something – as if I wasn't quite a complete human being. The phrase *only child* stood there, pointing an accusatory finger at me. "Something's missing, pal," it told me.

In the world I lived in, it was accepted that only children were spoiled by their parents, weak and self-centred. This was a given – like the fact that the barometer goes down the higher up you go and the fact that cows give milk. That's why I hated it whenever someone asked me how many brothers and sisters I had. Just let them hear I didn't have any and instinctively they thought: *An only child, eh? Spoiled, weak and self-centred, I bet.* That kind of knee-jerk reaction depressed me, and hurt. But what depressed and hurt me more was something else: the fact that everything they thought about me was true.

In the six years I went to elementary school, I met just one other only child. So I remember her (yes, it was a girl) clearly. I got to know her well, and we talked about all sorts of things. We understood each other. You could even say I loved her.

Her last name was Shimamoto. Soon after she was born, she caught polio, which made her drag her left leg. On top of that, she'd transferred to our school at the end of fifth grade. Compared with me, then, she had a terrible load of psychological baggage to struggle with. This baggage, though, had made her a tougher, more self-possessed only child than I could ever have been. She never whined or complained, never gave any indication of the irritation she must have felt at times. No matter what happened, she'd manage a smile. The worse things got, in fact, the broader her smile became. I loved her smile. It soothed me, encouraged me. *It'll be all right*, her smile told me. *Just hang in there, and everything will be OK.* Years later, whenever I thought of her, it was her smile that came to my mind first.

Shimamoto was kind to everyone. People respected her. In this sense she and I were different, although we were both only children. This doesn't mean that everyone in our class liked her. No one teased her or made fun of her, but, except for me, she had no real friends.

She was probably too cool, too self-possessed. Some of the others in our class must have thought her cold and haughty. But I detected something else – something warm and fragile just below the surface. Something very much like a child playing hide-and-seek, hidden deep within her, yet hoping to be found.

Because her father was transferred within his company a lot, Shimamoto had been to quite a few schools. I can't remember what her father did. Once, she explained to me in detail what his work was, but as with most kids, it went in one ear and out the other. I seem to recall some professional job connected with a bank or tax office or something. She lived in company housing, but the house was larger than normal, a Western-style house with a low, solid, stone wall surrounding it. Above the wall was an evergreen hedge and through gaps in it you could catch a glimpse of a garden with a lawn.

Shimamoto was a large girl, about as tall as I was, with striking features. I was certain that in a few years she would be gorgeous. But when I first met her she hadn't developed an outer look to match her inner qualities. Something about her was unbalanced, and not many people felt she was much to look at. There was an adult part of her and a part that was still a child – and they were out of sync. And this made people uneasy.

Probably because our houses were so close, literally a stone's throw from each other, the first month after she came to our school she was assigned to the seat next to mine. I told her what textbooks she'd need, what the weekly tests were like, how much we'd covered in each book, how the cleaning and the serving-lunch assignments were handled. Our school's policy was for the child who lived nearest any new student to help him or her out; my teacher took me aside to tell me that he expected me to take special care of Shimamoto, with her lame leg.

As with all kids of eleven or twelve talking to a member of the opposite sex for the first time, for a couple of days our conversations were strained. When we found out we were both only children, though, we relaxed. It was the first time either of us had met another only child. We both had so much we'd held inside about being only children. Often we'd walk home together. Slowly, because of her leg, we'd walk the three-quarters of a mile home, talking about all kinds of things. The more we talked, the more we realized what we had in common: our love of books and music; not to mention cats. We both had a hard time explaining our feelings to others. We both had a long list of foods we didn't want to eat. When it came to subjects at school, we had no trouble concentrating on the ones we liked; the ones we disliked we hated to death. But there was one major difference between us – more than I did, Shimamoto consciously wrapped herself in a protective shell. Unlike me, she made an effort to study the subjects she hated, and she got good marks. When the school dinner contained food she loathed, she still ate it. In other words, she constructed a much taller defensive wall around herself than I ever built. What remained behind that wall, though, was much the same as what lay behind mine.

Unlike times when I was with other girls, I could relax with Shimamoto. I loved going home with her. She limped slightly as she walked. We sometimes had a rest on a park bench halfway home, but I didn't mind. Rather the opposite – I was glad to have the extra time.

Soon we began to spend a lot of time together, but I don't recall anyone teasing us about it. This didn't strike me at the time, though now it seems strange. After all, kids that age naturally make fun of any couple who seem close. It might have been because of the kind of person Shimamoto was. Something about her made other people tense. She had an air that made people think: *Whoa – I'd better not say anything too stupid in front of this girl.* Even our teachers were some-what on edge when dealing with her. Maybe her lameness had something to do with it. At any rate, most people thought Shimamoto was not the sort of person you teased, and that was fine with me.

During PE she sat on the sidelines, and when our class went hiking or mountain climbing she stayed at home. Same with summer swimming camp. On our annual sports day, she did seem a little out of sorts. But other than this, her school life was typical. Hardly ever did she mention her leg. If memory serves, not even once. Whenever we walked home from school together, she never once apologized for holding me back or let this thought graze her expression. I knew, though, that it was precisely because her leg bothered her that she refrained from mentioning it. She didn't like to go to other kids' homes much, since she'd have to remove her shoes, Japanese style, at the entrance. The heels of her shoes were different heights, and the shoes themselves were shaped differently – something she wanted at all costs to conceal. They must have been made-to-measure. When she arrived at her own home, the first thing she did was toss her shoes in the cupboard as fast as she could.

Shimamoto's house had a brand-new stereo in the living room, and I used to go over there to listen to music. It was a nice stereo. Her father's LP collection, though, didn't do it justice. At most he had fifteen records, chiefly collections of light classics. We listened to those fifteen records a thousand times, and even today I can recall the music – every single note.

Shimamoto was in charge of the records. She'd take one from its sleeve, place it carefully on the turntable without touching the grooves with her fingers, and, after making sure to clean the cartridge of any dust with a tiny brush, lower the needle ever so gently on to the record. When the record was finished, she'd spray it and wipe it with a felt cloth. Finally she'd return the record to its sleeve and its proper place on the shelf. Her father had taught her this procedure, and she followed his instructions with a terribly serious look on her face, her eyes narrowed, her breath held in check. Meanwhile, I sat on the sofa, watching her every move. Only when the record was safely back on the shelf did she turn to me and give a little smile. And every time, this thought hit me: it wasn't a record she was handling, it was a fragile soul inside a glass bottle.

In my house we didn't have records or a record player. My parents didn't care much for music. So I was always listening to music on a small plastic AM radio. Rock and roll was my favourite, but before long I grew to enjoy Shimamoto's brand of classical music. This was music from another world, which had its appeal, but more than that I loved it because *she* was a part of that world. Once or twice a week, she and I would sit on the sofa, drinking the tea her mother made for us, and spend the afternoon listening to Rossini overtures, Beethoven's "Pastorale", and the *Peer Gynt* Suite. Her mother was happy for me to be there. She was pleased her daughter had a friend so soon after transferring to a new school, and I suppose it helped that I was neatly dressed. Honestly, I couldn't bring myself to like her mother very much. There was no particular reason I felt that way. She was always nice to me, but I could detect a hint of irritation in her voice and it put me on edge.

Of all her father's records, the one I liked best was a recording of the Liszt piano concertos: one concerto on each side. I liked it for two reasons. First of all, the record sleeve was beautiful. Second, no one I knew – with the exception of Shimamoto, of course – ever listened to Liszt's piano concertos. The very idea excited me. I'd found a world that no one around me knew – a secret garden only I was allowed to enter. I felt elevated, lifted to another plane of existence.

And the music itself was wonderful. At first it struck me as exaggerated, artificial, even incomprehensible. Little by little, though, with repeated listenings, a vague image formed in my mind – an image that had meaning. When I closed my eyes and concentrated, the music came to me as a series of whirlpools. One whirlpool would form and out of it another would take shape. And the second whirlpool would connect up with a third. Those whirlpools, I realize now, had a conceptual, abstract quality to them. More than anything, I wanted to tell Shimamoto about them. But they were beyond ordinary language. An entirely different set of words was needed, but I had no idea what they were. What's more, I didn't know if what I was feeling was worth putting into words. Unfortunately, I can't remember the name of the pianist now. All I recall are the colourful, vivid record sleeve and the weight of the record itself. The record was hefty and thick in a mysterious way.

The collection in her house included one record each by Nat King Cole and Bing Crosby. We listened to those two a lot. The Crosby one featured Christmas songs, which we enjoyed regardless of the season. It's strange how we could enjoy something like that over and over again.

One December day near Christmas, Shimamoto and I were sitting in her living room. On the sofa, as usual, listening to records. Her mother was out of the house on some errand, and we were alone. It was a cloudy, dark winter afternoon. The sun's rays, streaked with fine dust, barely shone through the heavy layer of clouds. Everything looked dim and motion-less. It was nearing twilight, and the room was as dark as night. A paraffin heater bathed the room in a faint glow. Nat King Cole was singing "Pretend". Of course, we had no idea then what the English lyrics meant. To us they were more like a chant. But I loved the song and had heard it so many times I could imitate the opening lines:

> Pretend you're happy when you're blue
> It isn't very hard to do

The song and the lovely smile that always graced Shimamoto's face were one and the same to me. The lyrics seemed to express a certain way of looking at life, though at times I found it hard to see life in that way.

Shimamoto had on a blue sweater with a round neck. She owned a fair number of blue sweaters; it must have been her favourite colour. Or maybe she wore those sweaters because they went well with the navy-blue coat she always wore to school. The white collar of her blouse peeped out at her throat. A check skirt and white cotton socks completed her outfit. Her soft, tight sweater revealed the slight swell of her breasts. She sat on the sofa with both legs folded underneath her. One elbow resting on the back of the sofa, she stared at some far-off, imaginary scene as she listened to the music.

"Do you think it's true what they say – that parents of only children don't get on very well?" she asked.

I mulled over the idea. But I couldn't work out its cause and effect.

"Where did you hear that?" I asked.

"Somebody said that to me. A long time ago. Parents who don't get on very well end up having only one child. It made me so sad when I heard that."

"Hmm . . . " I said.

"Do your mother and father get on all right?"

I couldn't answer right away. I'd never thought about it before.

"My mother isn't too strong physically," I said. "I'm not

11

sure, but it was probably too much of a strain for her to have another child after me."

"Have you ever wondered what it would be like to have a brother or sister?"

"No."

"Why not?"

I picked up the record sleeve on the table. It was too dark to read what was written on it. I put it down and rubbed my eyes a couple of times with my wrist. My mother had once asked me the same question. The answer I gave then didn't make her happy or sad. It just puzzled her. But for me it was a totally honest, totally sincere answer.

The things I wanted to say got all jumbled up as I talked and my explanation seemed to go on for ever. But what I was trying to get across was this: the me that's here now has been brought up without any brothers or sisters. If I did have brothers or sisters I wouldn't be the me I am. So it's unnatural for the me that's here before you to think about what it would be like to have brothers or sisters . . . In other words, I thought my mother's question was pointless.

I gave the same answer to Shimamoto. She gazed at me steadily as I talked. Something about her expression pulled people in. It was as if – this is something I thought of only later, of course – she were gently peeling back, one after another, the layers that covered a person's heart, a very sensual feeling. Her lips moved ever so slightly with each change in her expression, and I could catch a glimpse deep within her eyes of a faint light, like a tiny candle flickering in the dark, narrow room.

"I think I understand what you mean," she said in a mature, quiet voice.

"Really?"

"Um," she answered. "There are some things in this world

12

that can be changed and some that can't. And time passing is one thing that can't be redone. Come this far and you can't go back. Don't you think so?"

I nodded.

"After a certain length of time has passed, things harden. Like cement in a bucket. And we can't go back any more. What you want to say is that the cement that makes you up has set, so the you you are now can't be anyone else."

"I guess that's what I mean," I said uncertainly.

Shimamoto looked at her hands for a time.

"Sometimes, you know, I start thinking. About after I grow up and get married. I think about what kind of house I'll live in, what I'll do. And I think about how many children I'll have."

"Wow," I said.

"Haven't you ever thought about that?"

I shook my head. How could a twelve-year-old boy be expected to think about that? "So how many kids do you want to have?"

Her hand, which up till then had lain on the back of the sofa, she now placed on her knee. I stared vacantly at her fingers tracing the plaid pattern of her skirt. There was something curious about it, as if invisible thread emanating from her fingertips was spinning together an entirely new concept of time. I closed my eyes, and in the darkness, whirlpools flashed before me. Countless whirlpools were born and disappeared without a sound. Off in the distance, Nat King Cole was singing "South of the Border". The song was about Mexico, but at the time I had no idea. The words "south of the border" had a strange, appealing ring to them. I was convinced something utterly wonderful lay south of the border. When I opened my eyes, Shimamoto was still moving her fingers along her skirt. Somewhere deep inside my body I felt an exquisitely sweet ache.

"It's strange," she said, "but when I think about children, I can only imagine having one. I can somehow picture myself having children. I'm a mother and I have a child. I have no problem with that. But I can't picture that child having any brothers or sisters. It's an only child."

She was, without a doubt, a precocious girl. I feel sure she was attracted to me as a member of the opposite sex – a feeling I reciprocated. But I had no idea how to deal with those feelings. Shimamoto didn't, either, I suspect. We held hands just once. She was leading me somewhere and grabbed my hand as if to say, *This way – hurry up.* Our hands were clasped together for ten seconds at most, but to me it felt more like thirty minutes. When she let go of my hand, I was suddenly lost. It was all very natural, the way she took my hand, but I knew she'd been dying to.

The feel of her hand has never left me. It was different from any other hand I'd ever held, different from any touch I've ever known. It was merely the small, warm hand of a twelve-year-old girl, yet those fingers and that palm were like a display case crammed full of everything I wanted to know – and everything I *had* to know. By taking my hand, she showed me what these things were. That within the real world a place like this existed. In the space of those ten seconds I became a tiny bird, fluttering into the air, the wind rushing by. From high in the sky I could see a scene far away. It was so far off I couldn't make it out clearly, yet something was there and I knew that some day I would travel to that place. This revelation made me catch my breath and made my chest tremble.

I returned home and, sitting at my desk, I gazed for a long time at the fingers Shimamoto had clasped. I was ecstatic that she'd held my hand. Her gentle touch warmed my heart for days. At the same time it confused me, made me perplexed, even sad in a way. How could I possibly come to terms with that warmth?

When we left elementary school, Shimamoto and I went on to separate junior highs. I moved from the home I had lived in till then to a new town. I say a new town, but it was only two stops on the train from where I grew up, and in the first three months after I moved I went to see her three or four times. But that was it. Finally I stopped going. We were both at a delicate age, when the mere fact that we went to different schools and lived two train stops apart was all it took for me to feel our worlds had changed completely. Our friends were different, so were our uniforms and textbooks. My body, my voice, my way of thinking, were undergoing sudden changes, and an unexpected awkwardness threatened the intimate world we had created. Shimamoto, of course, was going through even greater physical and psychological changes. And all of this made me uncomfortable. Her mother began to look at me in a strange way. *Why does this boy keep coming here?* she seemed to be saying. *He no longer lives in the neighbourhood, and he goes to a different school.* Maybe I was just being too sensitive.

So Shimamoto and I grew apart, and I ended up not seeing her any more. And that was probably (*probably* is the only word I can think of to use here; I don't consider it my job to investigate the expanse of memory called the past and judge what is correct and what isn't) a mistake. I should have stayed as close as I could to her. I needed her, and she needed me. But my self-consciousness was too strong, and I was too afraid of being hurt. I never saw her again. Until many years later, that is.

Even after we stopped seeing each other, I thought of her with great fondness. Memories of her encouraged me, soothed me, as I passed through the confusion and pain of adolescence. For a long time, she held a special place in my heart. I kept this special place just for her, like a "Reserved" sign on a quiet corner table in a restaurant. Despite the fact that I was sure I'd never see her again.

When I knew her I was still twelve years old, without any real sexual feelings or desire. Though I'll admit to a vaguely formed interest in the swell of her breasts and what lay beneath her skirt. But I had no idea what this meant, or where it might lead.

With ears perked up and eyes closed, I imagined the existence of a certain place. This place which I imagined was still incomplete. It was misty, indistinct, its outlines vague. Yet I was sure that something absolutely vital was waiting for me there. And I knew this: that Shimamoto was gazing at the same scene.

We were, the two of us, still fragmentary beings, just beginning to sense the presence of an unexpected, to-be-acquired reality that would fill us and make us whole. We stood in front of a door we'd never seen before. The two of us alone, beneath a glimmer of light, our hands tightly clasped together for a fleeting ten seconds of time.

2

In high school I was a typical teenager. This was the second stage of my life, a step in my personal evolution – abandoning the idea of being different, and settling for normality. Not that I didn't have my own problems. But what sixteen-year-old doesn't? Gradually I drew nearer to the world, and the world drew nearer to me.

By the time I was sixteen I wasn't a puny little only child any more. In junior high I started to go to swimming classes near my house. I mastered the crawl and went twice a week to swim lengths. My shoulders and chest filled out, and my muscles grew strong and taut. I was no longer the kind of sickly child who ran a temperature at the drop of a hat and took to his bed. Often I stood naked in front of the bathroom mirror, scrutinizing every nook and cranny of my body.

I could almost see the rapid physical changes right before my eyes. And I enjoyed them. I don't mean I was thrilled about becoming an adult. It was less the maturing process

I enjoyed than seeing the transformation in myself. I could be a new me.

I loved to read and to listen to music. I'd always liked books and my interest in them had been fostered by my friendship with Shimamoto. I started to go to the library, devouring every book I could lay my hands on. Once I began one, I couldn't put it down. Reading was like an addiction; I read while I ate, on the train, in bed until late at night, in school, where I'd keep the book hidden so I could read during class. Before long I bought a small stereo and spent all my time in my room, listening to jazz records. But I had almost no desire to talk to anyone about the experience I gained through books and music. I felt happy just being me and no one else. In that sense I could be called a stuck-up loner. I disliked all team sports. I hated any kind of competition where I had to score points against someone else. I much preferred to swim on and on, alone, in silence.

Not that I was a total loner. I managed to make some close friends at school, a few, at least. School itself I hated. I felt as though these friends were trying to crush me all the time and I had to always be prepared to defend myself. This toughened me. If it hadn't been for my friends, I would have emerged from those treacherous teenage years with even more scars.

After I started swimming, I was no longer so fussy about the food I ate, and I could talk to girls without blushing. I might be an only child, but no one gave it a second thought any more. At least on the outside, it seemed I had freed myself from the curse of the only child.

And I had a girlfriend.

She wasn't particularly pretty, not the type your mother would point out in the class photograph as the prettiest girl in school. But the first time I met her, I thought she was rather cute. You couldn't see it in a photo, but she had a straightforward warmth which attracted people. She wasn't the kind of beauty I could brag about. But I wasn't much of a catch, either.

She and I were in the same class in the junior year of high school and we went out on dates often. At first double dates, then just the two of us. For whatever reason, I always felt relaxed with her. I could say anything, and she would listen intently. I might just be gabbling away about some drivel, but from the expression on her face you'd have imagined I was revealing a magnificent discovery that would change the course of history. She was the first girl since Shimamoto to be fascinated by anything I had to say. And for my part, I wanted to know everything there was to know about her. What she ate every day, what kind of room she lived in. What she could see from her window.

Her name was Izumi. *Love your name*, I told her the first time we talked. "Mountain spring", it means in Japanese. *Throw in an axe, and out would pop a fairy*, I said, thinking of a fairy tale. She laughed. Izumi had a sister three years younger than her, and a brother five years younger. Her father was a dentist and they lived – no surprise – in a detached house, with a dog. The dog was an Alsatian named Karl, after Karl Marx, believe it or not. Her father was a member of the Japanese Communist Party. Granted there must be Communist dentists in the world, but the whole lot of them could probably fit into four or five buses. So I thought it was pretty weird that it was *my* girlfriend's father who happened to be one of this rare breed. Izumi's parents were tennis fanatics and every Sunday would find them, rackets in hand, heading off to the court. A Communist dentist tennis nut – what a weird combination! Izumi wasn't interested in politics, but she loved her parents and would join them for a game of tennis every so often. She tried to get me to play, but tennis wasn't my thing.

She envied me because I was an only child. She didn't get along well with her brother or sister. According to her, they were a couple of heartless idiots whom she wouldn't mind if she never saw again. I always wanted to be an only child, she said, living as I please, with no one bothering me every time I turn around.

On our third date I kissed her. She'd come round to my house that day. My mother was out shopping, so we had the place to ourselves. When I brought my face near and touched my lips to hers, she just closed her eyes and was silent. I'd prepared a dozen excuses in case she got angry or turned away, but I didn't need any of them. My lips on hers, I put my arms around her and drew her close. It was near the end of summer and she had on a seersucker dress. It was tied at the waist, and the tie hung loosely behind her like a tail. My hand touched the fastening of her bra. I could feel her breath on my neck. I was so excited my heart felt like it was going to leap out of my body. My penis was ready to burst; it pushed against her thigh, and she shifted a bit to one side. But that was all. She didn't seem upset.

We sat for some time on the sofa, holding each other tight. A cat was sitting on the chair opposite us. It opened its eyes, looked in our direction, stretched, and went back to sleep. I stroked her hair and put my lips to her tiny ears. I thought I should say something, but nothing came to me. I could barely breathe, let alone speak. I took her hand again, and kissed her once more. For a long time, the two of us were quiet.

After I saw her off at the station, I couldn't calm down. I went home and lay on the sofa and stared at the ceiling.

My mind was in a whirl. Finally my mother came home and said she'd get dinner ready. But food was the last thing I could think about. Without a word, I went out and wandered around the town for a good two hours. It was a strange feeling. I was no longer alone, yet at the same time I felt a deep loneliness I'd never known before. As with wearing glasses for the first time, my sense of perspective was suddenly transformed. Things far away I could touch and objects that once were hazy were now crystal clear.

When Izumi left me that day, she thanked me and told me how happy she was. She wasn't the only one. I couldn't believe a girl had actually let me kiss her. How could I not be ecstatic? Even so, I couldn't be unreservedly happy. I was like a tower that had lost its base. I was up high and the more I looked off into the distance, the dizzier I became. Why her? I asked myself. What do I know about her anyway? I'd met her a few times, talked a bit, that was all. I was jumpy, fidgety, out of control.

If it had been Shimamoto, there would be no confusion. Each of us, with no words spoken, would totally accept the other. No uncomfortable feelings, no unease. But Shimamoto was no longer around. She was in a new world of her own and so was I. Comparing Izumi and Shimamoto was pointless. The door that led to Shimamoto's world had slammed shut behind me and I needed to find my bearings in a new and different one.

I stayed up until the light shone faintly in the eastern sky. I slept for two hours, had a shower and went to school. I had to find Izumi and talk to her about what had happened between us. I wanted to hear from her lips that her feelings were unchanged. The last thing she'd said was how happy she was, but in the cold light of dawn it seemed more like an illusion I'd dreamed up. The day ended without my getting a chance to talk to her. At breaktime she was with her girl-friends, and when school finished she went straight home. Just once, when we were in the corridor changing classes, we managed to exchange glances. She beamed when she caught sight of me and I smiled back. That was all. But in her smile I caught an affirmation of the previous day's events. *It's all right*, her smile seemed to tell me. *Yesterday really did happen.* By the time I was on the train home, my confusion had gone. I wanted her and my desire won out over any doubts.

What I wanted was clear enough. Izumi naked, having sex with me. But that final destination was still a long way down the road. There was a certain order of events you had to follow. To arrive at sex, you first had to undo the zip of the girl's dress. And between zip and sex lay a process in which twenty – maybe thirty – subtle decisions and judgments had to be made.

First of all I had to get hold of some condoms. Actually, that step was a bit further down the chain of events, but I still had to get my hands on some. Never know when I might need them. But I couldn't just walk into a chemist's, plonk down some money and waltz out with a box of condoms. I'd never pass for anything other than what I was – a high-school junior – not to mention that I was too much of a coward to make the attempt. I could have tried one of the vending machines in the neighbourhood, but if anyone caught me red-handed, I'd be up the proverbial creek. For three or four days, I turned this quandary over in my mind endlessly.

In the end, things worked out more easily than I expected. I asked a precocious friend of mine, who was our local expert on these matters. *Look, the thing is,* I said to him, *I'd like to get some condoms, so what should I do? No sweat,* he deadpanned. *I can get you a whole box. My brother bought a ton of them through a catalogue. I don't know why he bought so many, but his cupboard's*

22

full of them. He'll never miss one box. Fantastic, I enthused. The next day he brought the condoms to school in a paper bag. I treated him to lunch and asked him not to breathe a word. *No problem,* he said. Of course he spilled the beans, told a couple of people I was in the market for condoms. These people told some others and it went round the school until Izumi heard about it. After school, she asked me to come up to the roof with her.

"Hajime, I heard you got some condoms from Nishida?" she asked. The word *condoms* didn't exactly roll off her tongue. She made it sound like the name of some infectious disease.

"Uh . . . yeah," I admitted. I struggled to find the right words. "It doesn't really mean anything. I just thought, you know, maybe it'd be better to have some."

"You got them because of me?"

"No, not really," I said. "I was just curious about what they were like. But if it bothers you, I'm sorry. I'll give them back, or throw them away."

We were sitting on a small stone bench in a corner of the roof. It looked like it might rain at any moment. We were all alone. It was completely still. I'd never known the roof to be so silent.

Our school was on a hilltop, and we had an unbroken view of the town and the sea. Once my friends and I stole some records from the Broadcast Club room and flung them off the roof – like frisbees; they sailed away in a beautiful arc. Off towards the harbour they flew, happily, as if life had been breathed into them for a fleeting instant. But finally one of them failed to get airborne and wobbled clumsily straight down on to the tennis court, where some startled first-year girls were practising their swings. It was detention for us. That had been more than a year before, and now here I was in the same spot, being grilled by my girlfriend about condoms.

I looked up and saw a bird etching a slow circle in the sky. Being a bird, I imagined, must be wonderful. All birds had to do was fly. No need to worry about contraception.

"Do you really like me?" Izumi asked me in a small voice.

"Of course I do," I replied. "Of course I like you."

Lips pursed, she looked straight into my face. She looked at me for so long it made me uneasy.

"I like you too, you know," she said after a while.

But, I thought.

"But," she said, sure enough, "there's no need to rush."

I nodded.

"Don't be too impatient. I have my own pace. I'm not that clever a person. I need lots of time to prepare for things. Can you wait?"

Once again I nodded silently.

"Promise?" she asked.

"I promise."

"You won't hurt me?"

"I won't hurt you."

She looked down at her shoes for a while. Plain black loafers. Compared to mine, lined up next to them, they were as tiny as toys.

"I'm scared," she said. "These days I feel like a snail without a shell."

"I'm scared too," I said. "I feel like a frog without webbed feet."

She looked up and smiled.

Wordlessly we walked over to a shaded part of the building and held each other and kissed, a shell-less snail and a web-less frog. I held her close to me. Our tongues met lightly. I felt her breasts through her blouse. She didn't resist. She just closed her eyes and sighed. Her breasts were small and fitted comfortably in the palm of my hand, as if designed solely for that purpose. She placed her palm above my heart, and the feel of her hand and the beat of my heart became one. She's not Shimamoto, I told myself. She can't give me what Shimamoto gave. But here she is, all mine, trying her best to give me all she can. How could I ever hurt her?

But I didn't understand then. That I could hurt somebody so badly she would never recover. That a person can, just by living, damage another human being beyond repair.

3

Izumi and I went out together for more than a year. We went out once a week, to a film, or we studied together at the library, or we just went for long, aimless walks. As far as sex goes, though, we never made it all the way. About twice a month she came over to my house when my parents were out and we held each other on my bed. But she never took all her clothes off. *You never know when someone might come back*, she insisted. Overly cautious, you could call her. She wasn't scared; she just hated to be pushed into a potentially embarrassing situation.

So I always had to hold her with her clothes on and fumble around as best I could beneath her underwear.

"Slow down," she told me whenever my disappointment showed. "I need more time. Please."

Actually, I wasn't in that much of a rush myself. I was just confused, and disappointed by all sorts of things. Of course, I liked her and was grateful that she was my girlfriend. If she hadn't been with me, my teenage years would have been stale and colourless. She was basically an honest, pleasant girl, someone people liked. But our interests were worlds apart. She couldn't understand the books I read or the music I listened to, so we couldn't talk as equals about them. In this sense, my relationship with her differed dramatically from that with Shimamoto.

But when I sat beside her and touched her fingers, a natural warmth welled up inside me. I could tell her anything. I loved kissing her eyelids and just above her lips. I also liked to push her hair up and kiss her tiny ears, which invariably sent her into fits of giggles. Even now, whenever I think of her, I picture a quiet Sunday morning. A gentle, clear day, just getting under way. No homework to do, just a Sunday when you could do what you wanted. She always gave me this lie-back-and-relax, Sunday-morning kind of feeling.

Of course, she had her faults. She was pretty hard-headed and could have done with a bit more in the imagination department. She wasn't about to take even one step outside the comfortable world she had been brought up in. She never got so involved in something that she totally forgot about eating and sleeping. And she loved and respected her parents. The opinions she did put forth – the standard opinions of a sixteen-, seventeen-year-old girl – were, not surprisingly, insipid. On the plus side, I never once heard her bad-mouth another person. And she never bored me with conceited talk. She liked me and was good to me. She listened carefully to what I had to say and cheered me up. I talked a lot about myself and my future, what I wanted to become, the kind of person I hoped to be. A young boy's narcissistic fairy tales. But she listened intently. "I know you'll be a wonderful person when you grow up. There is something special about you," Izumi told me. And she was serious. No one had ever told me that before.

And holding her – even with her clothes on – was fantastic. What confused and disappointed me, though, was that I could never discover within her something special that existed just for me. A list of her good qualities far outstripped a list of her faults and certainly far outshone my own, yet there was something missing, something which was vital. If only I'd been able to pin down what that was, I know we would have ended up sleeping together. I wouldn't have held back for ever. Even if it had taken a long time, I would have persuaded her that it was absolutely necessary for her to sleep with me. But I lacked the confidence to see this through. I was just a rash seventeen-year-old whose head was crammed full of lust and curiosity. But in that head of mine I still knew that if she didn't want to have sex, I shouldn't try to force the issue. I had to wait patiently for the right time.

I did, though, hold Izumi naked in my arms once. I can't stand holding you with your clothes on, I pleaded. If you don't want to have sex, that's OK. But I want to see your body, I want to hold you with nothing on. I *have* to, and I can't bear it any longer.

Izumi thought for a while and then said that if it was what I really wanted, she didn't mind. "But promise me, OK," she looked at me seriously, "that's all you'll do? Don't do anything I don't want to."

She came over to my house on a beautiful, clear Sunday at the beginning of November. A bit chilly, though. My parents had to go to a memorial service for someone on my father's side of the family, and I should really have gone with them. I told them I had to study for a test, and stayed at home alone. They weren't due back until that night. Izumi came over in the afternoon. We held each other in my bed and I took her clothes off. She closed her eyes and let me undress her. It wasn't easy. I'm all thumbs, to begin with, and girls' clothes are a pain. Halfway through, Izumi opened her eyes and took over. She had on light-blue knickers and a matching bra. She had probably bought these specially for the occasion; up till then her underwear was always the kind mothers bought their high-school-age girls. Finally I undressed myself.

I held her naked body and kissed her neck and breasts. I stroked her smooth skin and breathed in its fragrance. Holding each other, naked like this, was out of this world. I felt if I didn't go inside her I'd go insane. But she pushed me firmly away.

"I'm sorry," she said.

Instead, she took my penis in her mouth and licked it all over. She'd never done that before. Over and over she drew her tongue over the tip of my penis, until I couldn't think straight and I came.

Afterwards, I held her close, caressing every inch of her body. Bathed in the autumn light, her body was beautiful and I kissed her all over. It was truly a gorgeous afternoon. We held each other tight many times, and I came again and again. Each time I came, she went to the bathroom to rinse her mouth.

"What a weird sensation." She laughed.

I had been going out with Izumi for just over a year, but that was without a doubt the happiest time we ever spent together. Naked, we had nothing to hide. I felt I knew more about her than ever before, and she must have felt the same. What we needed were not words and promises but the steady accumulation of small realities.

Izumi lay still for a long while, her head nestled on my chest as if she were listening to my heartbeat. I stroked her hair. I was seventeen, healthy, on the verge of becoming an adult. Wonderful is the only word for it.

Around four, just as she was getting dressed to leave, the doorbell rang. At first I just ignored it. I had no idea who it was; if I didn't answer it, whoever it was would surely give up and go away. But the doorbell rang on insistently. Damn, I thought.

"Are your parents back?" Izumi asked, blanching. She was out of bed, hurriedly gathering up her clothes.

"Don't worry. They can't be home this early. And they have a key, so they wouldn't ring the bell."

"My shoes!" she said.

"Shoes?"

"My shoes are just inside the front door."

I threw on my clothes, rushed downstairs and tossed her shoes inside the hall cupboard. When I opened the door, my aunt was standing there. My mother's younger sister, who lived about an hour's train ride away and visited us every so often.

"What on earth were you doing? I've been ringing the bell for ever," she said.

"I was listening to music with headphones on so I didn't hear you," I replied. "My parents are out – they went to a memorial service. They won't be back till late tonight. I suppose you know that, though."

"They told me. I had something to do in the neighbourhood and I knew you were at home studying, so I thought I'd cook supper for you. I've already shopped."

"I can make supper myself. I'm not a child, you know," I said.

"But I've bought everything. And you're busy, aren't you? I'll just make supper while you study."

Oh God, I thought. I wanted to curl up and die. Now how was Izumi going to get home? In my house you had to go through the living room to get to the front door, then pass the kitchen window to get to the gate. Of course, I could introduce Izumi as a friend who came over to see me, but I was supposed to be studying hard for an exam. If it came out that I'd had a girl round, there'd be hell to pay. I couldn't very well ask my aunt to keep it a secret from my parents. My aunt wasn't a bad person, but keeping secrets was not one of her strong points.

While my aunt was in the kitchen getting her shopping out of the bags, I took Izumi's shoes upstairs. She was fully dressed. I explained the situation.

She turned pale. "What on earth am I supposed to do? What if I can't get out of here? You know I have to be home every night by dinnertime. If I'm not, I'll be in big trouble."

"Don't worry. It'll be OK. We'll figure something out," I said, trying to calm her down. But in fact I was just as clueless about the next step.

"And I can't find one of my suspenders. I've looked everywhere."

"Your suspender?" I asked.

"A little metal thing, about this big."

I scoured the room, from the floor to the top of my bed. But I couldn't find it.

"Sorry. Couldn't you leave your stockings off just this once?" I asked.

I went into the kitchen, where my aunt was chopping vegetables. We need some vegetable oil, she said and asked me to go out to buy some. I couldn't refuse, so I rode my bike over to a nearby shop. It was already growing dark outside. At this rate Izumi might be stuck in my house for ever. I had to do something before my parents got home.

"I think our only chance is for you to slip out while my aunt's in the loo," I told Izumi.

"Do you think it'll work?"

"Let's give it a shot. We can't sit around like this, twiddling our thumbs."

I'd wait downstairs till my aunt went to the loo; then clap my hands twice loudly. Izumi would come downstairs, put on her shoes, and leave. If she made her escape all right, she would call me from a nearby pay phone.

My aunt sang happily as she sliced vegetables, made miso soup, and fried up some eggs. But no matter how much time passed, she didn't go to the loo. For all I knew, she might be listed in the *Guinness Book of Records*, under World's Biggest Bladder. I was about to give up, when she took off her apron and left the kitchen. As soon as I saw she was in the loo, I raced to the living room and clapped twice, hard. Izumi tiptoed downstairs, shoes in hand, quickly slipped them on, and as quietly as she could crept out of the front door. I went to the kitchen to make sure that she got out of the front gate. A second later, my aunt came out of the bathroom. I breathed a sigh of relief.

Five minutes afterwards, Izumi called me. Telling my aunt I'd be back in fifteen minutes, I went out. Izumi was standing in front of the payphone.

"I *hate* this," she said before I could get out a word. "I don't *ever* want to do this again."

I couldn't blame her for being angry and upset. I led her to the park near the station and sat her down on a bench. And gently held her hand. Over her red sweater she had on a beige coat. I recalled fondly what lay beneath.

"But today was beautiful. I mean until my aunt showed up. Don't you think so?" I asked.

"Of course I enjoyed it. Every time I'm with you I have a wonderful time. But every time, afterwards, I get confused."

"About what?"

"The future. After I leave high school you'll go to university in Tokyo, and I'll stay here. What's going to happen to us?"

I'd already decided to go to a college in Tokyo after I left high school. I was dying to get out of my home town, to live on my own away from my parents. My overall performance wasn't that great, but in the subjects I did like I got pretty good marks without opening a book, so getting into a private college would be no big deal, since their exams covered only a couple of subjects. But there was no way Izumi would be joining me in Tokyo. Her parents wanted to keep her close at hand, and she wasn't the rebellious type. So she wanted me to stay put. We have a good college here, she argued. Why do you have to go all the way to Tokyo? If I had promised not to leave, I'm sure she would have slept with me.

"Come on," I said. "It's not as if I'm going off to a foreign country. It's only three hours away. And college vacations are long, so for three or four months of the year I'll be here." I'd explained it to her a dozen times.

"But if you leave here you'll forget all about me. And you'll find another girlfriend," she said. I'd heard these lines at least a dozen times too.

I told her that wouldn't happen. I like you a lot, I said, so how can I forget you that easily? But I wasn't so sure. A simple change of scenery can bring about powerful shifts in the flow of time and emotions: exactly what had happened to Shimamoto and me. We might have been very close, but moving down the road a couple of miles was all it took for us to go our separate ways. I liked her a lot, and she told me to come and see her. But in the end I stopped going.

"There's one thing I just can't understand," Izumi said. "You say you like me. And you want to take care of me. But sometimes I can't figure out what's going on inside your head."

Izumi took a handkerchief from her coat pocket and wiped away her tears. With a start, I realized she'd been crying for some time. I had no idea what to say, so I sat and waited for her to continue.

"You prefer to think things over all by yourself and you don't like people looking inside your head. Maybe that's because you're an only child. You're used to thinking and acting alone. You figure that as long as *you* understand something, that's enough." She shook her head. "And that makes me afraid. I feel abandoned."

Only child. I hadn't heard those words in a long while. In elementary school the words had hurt me. But Izumi was using them in a different sense. Her "only child" didn't mean a pampered, spoiled kid but spoke to my isolated ego, which kept the world at arm's length. She wasn't blaming me. The situation just made her very sad.

"I can't tell you how happy I was when we held each other. It gave me hope, and I thought, who knows, maybe everything *will* work out," she said as we said goodbye. "But life isn't that easy, is it."

On the way back from the station, I mulled over what she'd said. It made sense. I wasn't used to opening up to others. She was opening up to me, but I couldn't do the same. I really did like her, yet still something held me back.

I'd walked home from the station a thousand times, but now it was like a foreign town. I couldn't shake off the image of Izumi's naked body: her taut nipples, her wisp of pubic hair, her soft thighs. And eventually I couldn't stand it any longer. I bought some cigarettes from a vending machine, went back to the park where we'd talked and lit a cigarette to calm down.

If only my aunt hadn't barged in on us, things might have worked out better. If nothing had disturbed us, we could have had a pleasanter goodbye. We would have been even happier. But even if my aunt hadn't arrived, someday something similar was bound to happen. If not today, then tomorrow. The biggest problem was that I couldn't convince her this was inevitable. Because I couldn't convince myself.

As the sun set, the wind grew cold. Winter was fast approaching. And when the new year came, there would be entrance exams and the beginning of a brand-new life. Uneasy though I was, I yearned for change. My heart and body both craved this unknown land, a blast of fresh air. That was the year Japanese universities were taken over by their students and Tokyo was engulfed in a storm of demonstrations. The world was transforming itself before my eyes, and I was dying to catch that fever. Even if Izumi wanted me to stay and would have sex with me to ensure that, I knew my days in this sleepy town were numbered. If that meant the end of our relationship, so be it. If I stayed here, something inside me would be lost for ever – something I couldn't afford to lose. It was like a vague dream, a burning, unfulfilled desire. The kind of dream people have only when they're seventeen.

Izumi could never understand my dream. She had her own dreams, a vision of a far different place, a world unlike my own.

But even before my new life began, a crisis came to rip our relationship to shreds.

4

The first girl I ever slept with was an only child. Like Izumi, she wasn't exactly the type to turn any heads; most people would hardly have noticed her. Still, the first time I laid eyes on her, it was as if I were walking down the road one afternoon and a silent bolt of lightning struck me smack on the head. No ifs, ands, or buts – I was hooked.

With a very few exceptions, typically beautiful women don't turn me on. Sometimes I'll be walking down the street and a friend will nudge me and say, "Wow! Did you see that girl?" But strangely enough, I can't recall a thing about this supposed knockout. And gorgeous actresses or models don't do a thing for me. I don't know why, but there it is. For me the boundary dividing the real world and the world of dreams has always been vague and whenever infatuation raised its almighty head, even during my early teens, a beautiful face wasn't enough to get me going.

I was always attracted not by some quantifiable, external

beauty, but by something deep down, something absolute. Just as some people have a secret love for rainstorms, earthquakes, or blackouts, I liked that certain undefinable *something* directed at me by members of the opposite sex. For want of a better word, call it magnetism. Like it or not, it's a power that ensnares people and reels them in.

The closest comparison might be the power of perfume. Perhaps even the master blender himself can't explain how a fragrance that has a special magnetism is created. Science certainly can't explain it. Still, the fact remains that a certain combination of fragrances can captivate the opposite sex like the scent of an animal in heat. One kind of fragrance might attract fifty out of a hundred people. And another scent will attract the other fifty. But there also are scents that only one or two people will find wildly exciting. And I have the ability, from far away, to sniff out those special scents. When I do, I want to go up to the girl who radiates this aura and say, *Look, I picked it up. No one else gets it, but I do.*

From the first time I saw this girl, I knew I wanted to sleep with her. More accurately, I knew I *had* to sleep with her. And instinctively I knew she felt the same way. When I was with her, my body, as the phrase goes, shook all over. And my penis got so hard I could barely walk. I'd probably felt the stirrings of this kind of attraction – a prototype of it – with Shimamoto, but I was too young to recognize it as such or even to give it a label. When I met this other girl, I was seventeen, a senior in high school, and she was twenty, in her second year at college. Of all things, she happened to be Izumi's cousin. She already had a boyfriend, but for the two of us that was beside the point. She could have been forty-two, with three kids and a pair of tails growing out of her backside, and I wouldn't have cared. The magnetism was that strong. I couldn't let this girl walk away. If I did, I would regret it for the rest of my life.

Anyway, that's how the person I lost my virginity with happened to be my girlfriend's cousin. And not just any old cousin, but the one she was closest to. Since they were little, Izumi and she had often visited each other. The cousin was at college in Kyoto and lived in an apartment near the west gate of Gosho, the old Imperial Palace. Izumi and I went to Kyoto once, so we phoned her and had lunch together. That was two weeks after the little farce with my aunt.

While Izumi was away for a few minutes, I asked her cousin for her telephone number, saying I'd like to ask her a few things about her college. Two days later, I called her and asked if I could see her the following Sunday. After a moment's pause, she said OK. Something in her tone of voice made me confident that she was hoping to sleep with me too. The following Sunday I went alone to Kyoto and met her, and by the afternoon, sure enough, we were in bed.

For the next two months we had such passionate sex I thought our brains were going to melt. No films, no walks, no small talk about novels, music, life, war, revolution. All we did was bang away. We must have talked a little, but I can't for the life of me recall what about. All I remember are detailed concrete images – the alarm clock near her pillow, the curtains on the windows, the black phone on the table, the photos on the calendar, and her clothes tossed aside on the floor. And the smell of her skin and her voice. I never asked any questions and she reciprocated. Just once, though, as we lay in bed, I suddenly wondered aloud whether she was, perhaps, an only child.

"That's right," she said, with a quizzical look. "But how did you know?"

"No particular reason. I just sensed it."

She looked at me for a while. "Maybe you're an only child too?"

"You've got it," I said.

That's all I remember about our conversations.

Only rarely did we stop to eat or drink. As soon as we laid eyes on each other, without a word exchanged between us, we'd yank off our clothes, hop into bed and get at it. I was greedy for what was before my eyes and so was she. Every time we met, we had sex four or five times, literally till my juices dried up and the tip of my cock swelled and ached. Despite the passion, and the violent attraction we each felt, it never occurred to either of us that we might want to become long-term lovers. We were in the midst of a whirl-wind that would, in time, pass. Knowing this, that each time we met might very well be the last, only fanned the flames of desire that much higher.

I wasn't in love with her. And she didn't love me. For me the question of love was irrelevant. What I sought was the sense of being tossed about by some raging, savage force, in the midst of which lay something absolutely crucial. I had no idea what that was. But I wanted to thrust my hand right inside her body and touch it, whatever it was.

I liked Izumi a lot, but not once did I experience that irrational power with her. I knew next to nothing about this other girl, yet her effect on me was profound. We never talked seriously about anything because we didn't see the point. If we'd had enough energy to talk, we'd have used it for another round between the sheets.

In the normal course of events we would have been wrapped up in our relationship, without pausing to come up for air, for a few months, and then one of us would have drifted away; the reason being that what we were doing was a necessary, natural act, one allowing no room for doubt. From

39

the first, there was no possibility that love, guilt, or thoughts of the future would enter in.

So if the relationship hadn't been discovered (not to have been found out seems pretty unrealistic, so totally wrapped up was I in having sex with her), Izumi and I might have continued for some time as we had, boyfriend and girlfriend. Whenever summer holidays came around, we'd have gone out together. Who knows how long the friendship would have lasted. But after a few years, one of us would have drifted away. We were too different, and time would only have magnified our differences. Looking back on it now, it all seems so obvious. Yet even if we had to go our separate ways, if I hadn't slept with her cousin we might have said goodbye as friends and moved on to the next stage of life in one piece.

As it turned out, we couldn't do this.

In truth, I damaged Izumi beyond repair. It didn't take much to realize how hurt she was. With her marks, she should have breezed into a top university, but she failed the entrance exam and ended up attending a small, third-rate girls' college. After my relationship with her cousin came to light, I saw Izumi only once. We talked for a long time in a coffee shop that had been one of our hangouts. I tried to explain things to her as honestly as I could, selecting my words carefully, straining to convey my feelings. This thing between me and your cousin wasn't planned, I said; it was a physical force that swept us off our feet. It didn't even leave me with the sense of guilt about betraying you that you'd expect me to have. It has nothing to do with *us*.

Of course, Izumi couldn't understand what I meant. And she called me a dirty liar. She was right on target. Without a word, I'd slept with her cousin behind her back. Not just once or twice, but ten, twenty times. I betrayed her from the word go. If I had been acting properly, after all, why the need for deception? I wanted to say this to Izumi: *I wanted to sleep with your cousin; I wanted to screw her till my brains fried – a thousand times, in every position imaginable. It has nothing to do with you*, I should have insisted from the start. But I couldn't. That's why I lied – repeatedly. I'd make up some excuse to break a date with her, then race down to Kyoto to screw her cousin. There was no getting around it – I was the one to blame.

Izumi found out about us near the end of January, not long after my eighteenth birthday. In February I sailed through all the college entrance exams and was going to move to Tokyo at the end of March. Before I left, I called her, over and over again. But she wouldn't come to the phone. I wrote her long letters, waiting in vain for a reply. I can't just leave like this, I thought. I can't just leave her here. But I was powerless. Izumi wanted nothing more to do with me.

On the bullet train to Tokyo, I gazed listlessly at the scenery outside and thought about myself – who I was. I looked down at my hands on my lap and at my face reflected in the window. *Who the hell am I?* I wondered. For the first time in my life, a fierce self-hatred welled up in me. How could I have done something like this? But I knew why. Put in the same position, I would do it all over again. Even if I had to lie to Izumi, I would sleep with her cousin. No matter how much it might hurt Izumi. Recognizing this was painful. But it was the truth.

Izumi wasn't the only one to be hurt. I hurt myself deeply, though at the time I had no idea how deeply. I should have learned many things from that experience, but when I look back on it, all I gained was one single, undeniable fact. That ultimately I am a person who can do evil. I never consciously tried to hurt anyone, yet good intentions notwithstanding,

41

when necessity demanded, I could become completely self-centred, even cruel. I was the kind of person who could, using some plausible excuse, inflict on a person I cared for a wound that would never heal.

College transported me to a new town, where I tried, once more, to reinvent myself. Becoming someone new, I could correct the errors of my past. At first I was optimistic: I could pull it off. But in the end, no matter where I went, I could never change. Over and over again I made the same mistake, hurt other people and hurt myself into the bargain.

Just after I turned twenty, this thought hit me: *Maybe I've lost the chance to ever be a decent human being.* The mistakes I'd committed – maybe they were part of my very make-up, an inescapable part of my being. I'd hit rock bottom and I knew it.

5

My four years of college were pretty much a waste of time. The first year I was in a few demonstrations and even fought the police. I was out there with the student strikers and showed up at political rallies. I met some wild characters that way, but my heart was never in politics. Linking arms with strangers at demonstrations made me uneasy and when we had to hurl stones at the cops I asked myself if this was really *me*. Was this what I wanted? I wondered. I couldn't feel the requisite solidarity with the people around me. The scent of violence that hung over the streets, the powerful slogans of the day, soon lost their point. And the time Izumi and I had spent together grew more precious in my mind. But there was no going back. I'd said farewell to that world.

Most of my classes were a complete bore. Nothing excited me. After a while, I was so busy with my part-time job that I hardly ever showed my face at college; luck alone allowed me to graduate in four years. When I was in the first year, I had a girlfriend I lived with for six months. But it didn't work out. I hadn't the foggiest idea what I wanted out of life.

The next thing I knew, the season of politics was over. Like a drooping flag on a windless day, the gigantic shock waves that had convulsed society for a time were swallowed up by a colourless, mundane, workaday world.

Once I had graduated, a friend helped me to get a job on the editorial staff of an educational publisher. I got a haircut, polished my shoes and bought a suit. It wasn't much of a company, but jobs for literature majors being few and far between that year, and considering my lousy marks and lack of connections, I had to settle for what I could get.

The job was a total bore. The company itself wasn't a bad place to work, but editing school textbooks didn't brighten my day one bit. At first I thought: *OK, I'll do my best, try to find something worthwhile in it*; and for half a year I worked as hard as I could. Give it all you've got, and something good's bound to happen, right? But I gave up. No matter how you looked at it, this wasn't the job for me. I felt as if the end of my life were staring me in the face. The months and years would drop away one by one, with me bored out of my skull. I had thirty-three years till retirement, chained day after day to a desk, staring at page proofs, counting lines, checking spelling. I'd get married to some nice girl, have some children, the usual twice-a-year bonus the one bright spot in an otherwise tedious existence. I remembered what Izumi had once told me. "I know you'll be a wonderful person when you grow up. There is something special about you." It pained me every time I remembered. *Something special about me, Izumi? Forget it. But I'm sure you know that now. Ah, what the hell, everyone makes mistakes.*

I did the work given to me mechanically and I spent my free time reading or listening to music. Work is just a boring obligation, I decided, and when I'm not working, I'm going to use my time the best way I can and enjoy myself. So I never went out drinking with the others at work. Not that I didn't get along with people. I just didn't make the effort to get to know my colleagues on a personal level. I was determined that my free time was going to be *mine*.

Four or five years passed in a flash. I had several girlfriends, but nothing lasted. I'd date one for a few months, and then start thinking: *This isn't what I want*. I couldn't find in these women something that was waiting just for me. I slept with a couple of them, but it was no big deal. I consider this to be the third stage of my life – the twelve years between my starting college and turning thirty. Years of disappointment and loneliness. And silence. Frozen years, when my feelings were shut up inside me.

I withdrew into myself. I ate alone, took walks alone, went swimming alone and went to concerts and the cinema alone. I didn't feel hurt or sad. I often thought of Shimamoto and of Izumi, and wondered where they were now, what they were doing. For all I knew, they might be married, even have children. I would have given anything to see them, to talk to them, even for an hour. With Shimamoto and Izumi, I could be honest. I racked my brains wondering how to get back together with Izumi, how to see Shimamoto again. I imagined how wonderful that would be. Not that I did anything to make it come true. The two of them were lost to me for ever. The hands of a clock run in only one direction. I started talking to myself, drinking alone at night. I was sure I would never get married.

Two years after I started work, I went out with a girl who had a bad leg. One of the men at work set me up with a double date.

"Something's wrong with one of her legs," he told me reluctantly. "But she's cute and has a great personality. I know you'll like her. And you won't really notice the leg. She just drags it a bit."

"Hey, it's not a problem," I replied. To be truthful, if he hadn't mentioned her bad leg, I would have turned him down. I was sick to death of double dates and blind dates. But when I heard about her leg, I somehow couldn't refuse.

You won't really notice the leg. She just drags it a bit.

The girl was a friend of the man's girlfriend. They had been friends at high school. She was on the small side, with decent looks. Hers was a subdued sort of beauty, reminding me of some small animal deep in the woods who seldom showed its face. The four of us went to the cinema one Sunday morning and then had lunch together. She hardly said a word. I tried my best to draw her out, but without any luck. She just smiled. Afterwards, we separated from the other couple. She and I went to take a walk in Hibiya Park, where we had some coffee. She dragged her right leg, not the left like Shimamoto. The way she twisted it, too, was different. Whereas Shimamoto rotated her leg slightly as she moved it forward, this girl pointed the tip sideways a bit and dragged it straight ahead. Still, their way of walking was remarkably similar.

She had on a red turtleneck sweater and jeans and a pair of desert boots. She wore hardly any make-up, and her hair was in a ponytail. Though she said she was in her last year at college, she looked younger. I couldn't decide if she was just a quiet person or if she was nervous meeting someone for the first time. Maybe she didn't have anything to talk about. Whatever, I wouldn't characterize our initial interaction as conversation. The only fact I was able to drag out of her was that she was at a private college, studying pharmacology.

46

"Pharmacology, huh? Is it interesting?" I asked. We were in the café in the park, having a cup of coffee.

She blushed.

"Hey, it's all right," I said. "Editing textbooks isn't exactly the world's most exciting activity. The world's full of boring things. Don't worry about it."

She thought for a while and at long last opened her mouth. "It's not that interesting. But my parents own a chemist's."

"Could you teach me something about pharmacology? I don't know the first thing about it. In the past six years I don't think I've swallowed a single pill."

"You're pretty healthy, then."

"I don't even get hangovers," I said. "When I was a kid, though, I was pretty sickly. Took lots of medicine. I was an only child, so my parents were overprotective."

She nodded, and stared into her coffee cup for a while. It was a long time before she spoke again.

"Pharmacology isn't the most thrilling subject," she began. "There have got to be a million things that are more fun than memorizing the ingredients of different medicines. It isn't romantic, like astronomy, or dramatic, like being a doctor. But there's something intimate about it, something I can feel close to. Something down-to-earth."

"I see," I said. She could talk, after all. It just took her longer than most to find the right words.

"Do you have any brothers or sisters?" I asked.

"Two older brothers. One's already married."

"So you're studying pharmacology because you'll be taking over the family shop?"

She blushed again. And was silent for a good long time. "I don't know. My brothers both have jobs, so maybe I will end up running the business. But nothing's decided. If I don't feel like it, that's OK, my father said. He'll run it for as long as he can, then sell it."

I nodded, and waited for her to continue.

"But I think maybe I should take it over. With this leg, it'd be hard to find another job."

So we talked and passed the afternoon together. With plenty of pauses, and long waits for her to continue. Whenever I asked her a question, she blushed. I enjoyed our conversation, which for me at the time was an accomplishment. Sitting there in the café with her, I felt something close to nostalgia well up in me. She began to feel like someone I'd known all my life.

Not that I was attracted to her. I wasn't. She was nice and I enjoyed our time together. She was a pretty girl and, as my friend said, quite pleasant. But all these good points aside, when I asked myself if there was something in her that would bowl me over, that would zoom straight to my heart, the answer was no. Nothing.

Only Shimamoto ever did that to me. There I was, listening to this girl and all the time thinking of Shimamoto. I knew I shouldn't be, but there it was. Just thinking of Shimamoto made me shiver all over, all these years later. A slightly fevered excitement, as if I were gently pushing open a door deep within me. Walking with this pretty girl with a bad leg through Hibiya Park, though, that kind of excitement, that all-over shivery feeling, was missing. What I did feel for her was a certain sympathy, and a calmness.

Her home – the chemist's, that is – was in Kobinata. I took her back on the bus. We sat side by side and she hardly said a word.

A few days later, my friend from work came over and told me the girl really seemed to like me. *On our next holiday*, he said, *why don't the four of us go somewhere together?* I made some excuse and bowed out. Not that I would have minded

48

seeing her again and talking to her. In fact, I wanted to have a chance to talk to her sometime. Under different circumstances we might have ended up good friends. But it started with a double date and the point of double dates is to find a partner. So if I did ask her out again, I'd be taking on a certain responsibility. And the last thing I wanted was to hurt her. All I could do was refuse.

I never saw her again.

6

During this period, one more woman with a lame leg figured
in a strange incident, whose meaning, even now, I can't
totally understand. I was twenty-eight when it happened.

I was in Shibuya, walking along in the end-of-year crowds,
when I spotted a woman dragging her leg exactly as Shimamoto used to do. She had on a long red overcoat and a black
patent-leather handbag was tucked under one arm. On her
left wrist she wore a silver watch, which was more like a
bracelet, really. Everything about her said money. I was on the
opposite side of the street, but when I saw her, I rushed over
at the intersection. The streets were so crowded it made me
wonder where all these people could possibly have come from,
but it didn't take me long to catch up with her. With her bad
leg, she walked fairly slowly, just like Shimamoto, rotating
her left leg as she dragged it along. I couldn't take my eyes off
the elegant curve inscribed by her beautiful stockinged legs,
the kind of elegance only long years of practice could produce.

I tailed her for a long while, staying a little way behind her. It wasn't easy keeping pace with her, walking at a speed the opposite of the crowd around. I adjusted my pace, stopping sometimes to look into a shop window, or pretending to rummage around in my pockets. She had on black leather gloves and carried a red department store carrier bag. Despite the overcast winter day, she wore a pair of sunglasses. From behind, all I could make out was her beautiful, neatly combed hair curled fashionably outwards at shoulder length, and her back tucked away in that soft, warm-looking red coat. Of course, if I really wanted to see if she was Shimamoto, I could have circled around in front and taken a good look at her. But what if it was Shimamoto? What should I say to her – and how should I act? She might not even remember me, for one thing. I needed time to pull myself together. I took some deep breaths to clear my head.

Taking care not to overtake her, I followed her for a long time. She never once looked back or stopped. She hardly glanced around her. She seemed to have a place to get to and was determined to get there as soon as she could. Like Shimamoto, she walked with her back erect and her head held high. Looking at her from the waist up, no one would ever have suspected that she had something wrong with her leg. She just walked more slowly than most people. The longer I looked at her, the more I remembered Shimamoto. If this wasn't Shimamoto, it had to be her twin.

The woman cut through the crowds in front of Shibuya Station and started up the slope in the direction of Aoyama. The hill slowed her down more. Still, she covered quite a bit of ground – so much I wondered why she didn't take a taxi. Even for someone with good legs, it was a long way. Yet on she walked, dragging her leg, with me following at a discreet distance. Nothing in any of the windows caught her eye.

51

She switched her handbag and her shopping bag from right to left a few times, but other than that she went on walking, never varying her pace.

Finally she left the crowded main street. She seemed to know the layout of the area well. One step away from the bustling shopping area, you entered a quiet residential street. I followed, taking even greater care not to be spotted in the thinned-out crowd.

I must have followed her for forty minutes. We went down the back street, turned several corners and once again emerged into the main thoroughfare. But she didn't join the flow of passers-by. Instead, as if she'd planned it all along, she went straight into a café which also sold cakes and sweets. I killed ten minutes or so sauntering back and forth, then went in after her.

It was stiflingly warm inside, yet she sat with her back to the door, still in her heavy overcoat. Her red overcoat couldn't be missed. I sat down at the table furthest from the entrance and ordered a cup of coffee. I picked up a newspaper lying on the table and, pretending to read, watched what she was doing. A cup of coffee sat on her table, but in all the time I watched her she didn't touch it. Once, she took a cigarette out of her handbag and lit it with a gold lighter, but other than that she just sat there, without moving, staring out of the window. She could have been taking a rest, or maybe she was deep in thought about some weighty matter. Sipping my coffee, I read the same article a dozen times.

After a long time, she stood up abruptly and headed right towards me. It happened so suddenly I felt as if my heart had stopped. But she wasn't coming over to me. She passed my table and went to the phone. Dropping in some coins, she dialled a number.

The phone wasn't far from where I was sitting, but with all

the loud conversations and Christmas carols booming out of the speakers, I couldn't hear what she was saying. She talked for a long time. Her coffee, untouched, grew cold. When she passed me, I could see her face from the front, but still I couldn't be absolutely sure if she was Shimamoto. She had on thick make-up, and half her face was hidden by those sunglasses. Her eyebrows were distinctly pencilled on, and her brightly outlined thin lips were drawn tightly together. Her face reminded me of Shimamoto as a young girl, but if someone had said it wasn't her, I would have believed them. After all, the last time I'd seen Shimamoto we were both twelve, and more than fifteen years had passed. All I could say for sure was that this was an attractive young woman in her twenties who had on an expensive outfit. And she had a bad leg.

Sweat rolled down me. My T-shirt was soaked. I took off my coat and ordered another cup of coffee. *Just what do you think you're doing?* I asked myself. I'd lost a pair of gloves and gone out to Shibuya to buy a replacement. But as soon as I caught sight of this woman, I was following her like someone possessed. Most people would have gone straight up to her and said, *"Excuse me, aren't you Miss Shimamoto?"* But I didn't. I said nothing and followed her. And I had finally come to the point where there was no turning back.

Finishing with her call, the woman went back to her seat. Just as before, she sat with her back to me, gazing at the scene outside. The waitress came up and asked if she could take her cold coffee away. I couldn't hear, but I think that's what she must have said. The woman turned around and nodded. And, it appeared, ordered another cup of coffee. When it came, though, again she didn't touch it. I continued to glance at the paper. Again and again she brought her wrist up to check the time on her silver watch, as if she

53

was waiting for someone impatiently. This might be my last chance, I told myself. If that other person shows up, I'll never be able to talk to her. But I remained rooted to my chair. It's still OK, I explained to myself. It's still OK, there's no need to rush.

Nothing happened for fifteen or twenty minutes. She kept gazing at the street scene outside. Suddenly, without warning, she stood up quietly, tucked her handbag under her arm, and picked up the carrier bag in one hand. She'd given up waiting, apparently. Or maybe she hadn't been waiting for anyone, after all. I watched as she paid her bill and left the café, then I stood quickly, paid my own bill and went after her. I could see her red overcoat making its way through the crowds. I followed her, weaving my way through the throng.

She had her hand up, trying to call a taxi. Finally one switched off it's light and pulled over to the curb. *I have to call out to her*, I thought. *If she gets in the taxi, it's all over*. Just as I stepped forward, though, someone grabbed my elbow. The powerful grip took my breath away. It didn't hurt, but the strength of the grip made me choke. I turned around, to find myself face to face with a middle-aged man, staring straight at me.

The man was a couple of inches shorter than me but powerfully built. In his mid-forties, I guessed. He had on a dark-grey overcoat and a cashmere scarf, both of which looked very expensive. His hair was neatly parted and he wore a pair of design tortoiseshell glasses. Seemingly into sport, he was nicely tanned. Skiing, I wondered. Or maybe tennis. I remembered how Izumi's father, who loved tennis, had the same sort of tan. This man looked like the executive of a prosperous firm, or maybe more like an important civil servant. His eyes told you that. The eyes of a man who was used to giving orders.

"Would you care for some coffee?" he asked quietly.

I followed the woman with my eyes. Bending down to get into the taxi, she glanced through her sunglasses in our direction. At least it seemed to me she looked our way. The taxi door closed and she disappeared from view, leaving me and this middle-aged stranger behind.

"I won't take much of your time," the man said, his tone of voice placid. He was neither angry nor excited. As though holding open a door for someone, he continued to grasp my arm tightly. "Let's have some coffee and talk."

I could have walked away. *I don't want any coffee and I have nothing to talk to you about. First of all, I don't know who you are, and I'm in a hurry, so if you'll excuse me,* I could have said. But I clammed up and just stared. Finally I nodded and did as he said, following him back into the café. Perhaps I was afraid of something in that powerful grip. I could feel a strangely immovable force there. More machine-like than human, his grip on me was perfect, never wavering in its pressure. If I had refused his suggestion, what would he have done to me? I couldn't imagine.

But as well as being scared, I was also half curious. I wanted to find out what he could possibly want to talk to me about. Maybe it would lead to some information about the woman. Now that she'd disappeared, this man might be the only link connecting her and me. Besides, the man wasn't about to beat me up in a café, was he?

We sat down at a table facing each other. Until the waitress came, we didn't say a word. We sat there, staring. The man ordered two coffees.

"Why, may I ask, were you following her for so long?" he asked me politely.

I couldn't answer.

With expressionless eyes, he looked long and hard at me.

"I know you were following her all the way from Shibuya," he said. "Follow someone that far and they're bound to catch on."

I didn't reply. She had realized I was following her, had gone into the café, and called this man.

"If you don't want to say anything, that's OK. I know what's going on without you having to tell me." He may have been worked up, but you couldn't tell from the polite, quiet way he spoke.

"There are several options here," the man said. "I'm not joking. Whatever I feel like doing, believe me, I can do."

Then he fell silent and continued to look at me. As if to give me the message that he didn't need an explanation, since he had the situation under control. As before, I said nothing. "But I don't want things to get out of hand. I don't want to cause a scene. Understand me? This time only," he said. He raised his right hand, which was lying on the table, reached into his inside pocket and took out a white envelope. All the while, his left hand remained on the table. It was nothing special, just a plain white business envelope. "Take this and don't say a word. I know someone put you up to this and I'd like to settle the matter amicably. Not a word about what's happened. Nothing special happened to you today, and you never met me. Understand? If I ever find out you've said anything, you can rest assured I will find you and take care of the matter. So I'd like you to forget about following her. Neither one of us wants any trouble. Correct?"

The man put the envelope in front of me and stood up. Snatching up the bill, he paid the cashier and strode out of the café. I sat there dumbfounded. Finally I picked up the envelope on the table and looked inside. There were ten ten-thousand-yen notes. Crisp, new, ten-thousand-yen notes. My mouth was parched. I shoved the envelope in my pocket and left the shop. I looked around, making sure that the man wasn't there, then hailed a taxi and went back to Shibuya, where this misadventure began.

Years later, I still had that envelope with the money. Without ever opening it again, I stuck it in a drawer in my desk. On nights when I couldn't sleep, I could see his face. Like an unlucky premonition of something, his face floated clearly into my mind. Who the hell *was* he anyway? And was that woman Shimamoto?

I came up with several theories. It was a puzzle without a solution. I would think of a hypothesis, only to shoot it down. The most convincing explanation was that this man was the woman's lover, who thought I was a detective hired by her husband to report on her activities. And the man thought his money would buy my silence. Maybe they thought I'd seen them both leaving a hotel where they'd had a rendezvous. It made sense. But even so, my gut feeling said no. Too many questions remained.

He said that if he wanted to, there were several things he could do to me, but what things did he mean? Why was he able to grab me in that unexpected way? If the woman knew I was following her, why didn't she hail a taxi? She could have lost me in a minute. And why did that man, not knowing who I really was, toss me an envelope full of so much money?

It continued to be a riddle. Sometimes I'd think it must have all been a delusion, from start to finish a fantasy I'd cooked up in my head. Or maybe a very long, realistic dream that somehow I'd mixed up with reality. But it did happen. Inside the drawer of my desk there was a white envelope with ten ten-thousand-yen notes inside, proof that it wasn't a dream. *It really happened.* Sometimes I put the envelope on top of my desk and stared at it. *It really did happen.*

7

I got married when I was thirty. I met my wife one summer holiday while I was travelling alone. She was five years younger than me. I was walking along a road in the country, when it suddenly started raining. I ducked into the nearest place I could find to get out of the storm, and she and a girlfriend were already there. All three of us were soaked to the skin and we started talking while we waited for the rain to stop. If it hadn't rained then, if I had taken an umbrella (which was entirely possible, since I had seriously debated doing so before I left the hotel), I would never have met her. And if I hadn't met her, I'd still be slaving away at the educational publisher's, still leaning against the wall in my flat at night, alone, drinking and babbling to myself. It makes me realize how limited our possibilities ever are.

Yukiko and I were attracted to each other from the beginning. Her friend was much prettier, but I only had eyes for

Yukiko. An irrationally strong attraction pulled us together; I'd nearly forgotten what that kind of magnetism felt like. She lived in Tokyo too, so after our return we went out together. The more I saw of her, the more I liked her. She was, if anything, on the plain side, at least not the type to attract men wherever she went. But there was something in her face that was meant for me alone. Every time we met, I took a good long look at her. And I loved what I saw.

"Why are you staring at me?" she'd ask.

"Because you're pretty," I'd reply.

"You're the first one who's ever said that."

"I'm the only one who knows," I'd tell her. "And believe me, I know."

At first she didn't believe me. But soon she did.

We'd go to some quiet place and talk. I could tell her anything, up front, no holds barred. I could feel the weight of all I had lost in those past ten years, all those years down the drain, bearing down on me. Before it was too late, I had to get some of it back. Holding Yukiko, I felt a nostalgic, long-gone thrill race through me. When we said goodbye, I was lost once again. Loneliness pained me, silence had me exasperated. A week before my thirtieth birthday, after we'd been going out together for three months, I proposed to her.

Her father was the president of a medium-sized construction company and a real character. He'd hardly been to school, yet he was an achiever – a bit too aggressive for my taste. Still, I was impressed by his unique outlook on life. I'd never met anybody like him. He drove around Tokyo in a chauffeur-driven Mercedes but he was never snobbish. When I went to see him to ask for his daughter's hand in marriage, he just said, "You're not children any more, so if you like each other it's up to you." I wasn't much of a catch, a nothing employee of a nothing company, but that didn't faze him.

Yukiko had an older brother and a younger sister. Her brother was vice president of the construction firm and was going to take it over. He wasn't a bad sort, but he was over-shadowed by his father. Of the three children, the younger sister, who was at college, was the most outgoing; she was used to getting her way. Come to think of it, she might have made a better president than her brother.

About six months after we were married, Yukiko's father asked me to come and see him. He'd heard from my wife that I wasn't too happy working for a publishing company, and he wanted to know if I was planning to leave my job.

"I have no problem with resigning," I said. "The problem is what I do after that."

"How about coming to work for me?" he asked. "I'll work you into the ground, but you won't beat the pay."

"Well, I know I'm not cut out for editing textbooks, but I don't think working in a construction firm's my thing, either," I said truthfully. "I appreciate the offer, but if I'm not interested in the work, the whole thing will end up being more bother than it's worth."

"You're probably right. Shouldn't force people to do what they don't want to do," he replied. It sounded as if he'd anticipated this answer. We were having a few drinks. His son hardly touched alcohol, so sometimes the two of us would drink together. "By the way, my company has a build-ing in Aoyama. It's under construction, should be finished next month. The location's good and it'll be quite a place. It's a little off the beaten track now, but the area's going to grow. I was thinking maybe you could open some kind of shop there. It's company property, so I'll have to take the going rate for the down payment and rent, but if you'd like to have a go at it, I can lend you as much as you want."

I thought about it for a while. The possibilities were intriguing.

That's how I came to open an upmarket jazz bar in the basement of a brand-new building in Aoyama. I had worked in a bar at college, so I was familiar with the ins and outs of running a drinking establishment – the kind of drinks and food you should serve, the music and atmosphere, the sort of clientèle to aim for, and so on. My father-in-law's company handled the interior decorating. He brought in a first-rate interior design firm and set them on to to it. Their price was surprisingly reasonable and when the bar was finished it was a sight to behold.

The bar was more successful than my wildest dreams, and two years later I opened a second one, also in Aoyama. This was a bigger place, featuring a live jazz trio. It took a lot of time and effort, not to mention a great deal of money, but I ended up with a popular and unique club. I'd done a reasonable job with the opportunity presented to me and I finally felt able to relax for a moment. Not coincidentally, this was when our first child, a girl, was born. At first I used to help out behind the counter, mixing cocktails, but after opening the second place, I was too busy with the business side. I had to make sure everything went smoothly – negotiating prices, hiring, keeping accounts. I even threw in my two pence worth regarding the menu. Surprisingly, I wasn't at all bad at this kind of work. I loved the process of starting from scratch, creating something, seeing it through till it was absolutely perfect. It was my bar, my own little world. Could you find this kind of happiness proofreading school textbooks? No way.

During the day I'd take care of all sorts of chores, then at night I'd make the rounds of my two bars, checking out the cocktails to see that they tasted right, watching the customers' reactions, making sure my employees were up to scratch. And I listened to the music. Each month I paid back some of what I owed my father-in-law; still, I was making a pretty good profit. Yukiko and I bought a four-bedroomed apartment in Aoyama and a BMW 320. And had a second child. Another girl. Before I knew what had hit me, I was the father of two little girls.

When I turned thirty-six, I bought a small cottage in Hakone and a red Jeep Cherokee for Yukiko to shop and ferry the children around in. With the profit from my bars I could have opened a third place, but I didn't plan to expand. Keeping track of all the details for two bars was enough; watching over any more would have left me exhausted. I was sacrificing enough time to work as it was. I discussed this with my wife's father and he suggested I put any extra money into stocks and property. It takes hardly any time or effort, he told me. But I knew absolutely nothing about the stock market or land. So he said, "Leave the details to me. If you do as I say, you'll do all right. There's a knack to these things." So I invested as he told me. And sure enough, in a short time I'd made a healthy profit.

"Now you get it, right?" he asked me. "There's a special knack to investing. You could work for a hundred years in a company and never end up doing this well. In order to succeed, you need luck and brains. Those are the basics. But they're not enough. You need capital. Not enough capital and your hands are tied. But above all, you need the *knack*. Without it, all those other things will get you nowhere."

"I suppose you're right," I said. I knew what he was getting at. The "knack" he talked about was the system he'd created. A tenacious, complex system for generating vast sums of money by building up an immense network of contacts,

62

gathering vital information and investing accordingly. Slipping through the net of laws and taxes, transfiguring itself in the process, the profit thus generated swelled almost beyond measure.

If I hadn't met my father-in-law, I'd still be editing textbooks. Still living in a lousy little flat in Nishiogikubo, still driving a used Toyota Corona with an air conditioner on the blink. Now, though, in a short space of time I found myself the owner of two bars in one of the smartest parts of town, employing more than thirty people and making more money than I'd ever made in my life – or ever dreamed of making. The business was running so well that even my accountant was impressed and the bars had a good reputation. I'm not saying I'm the only one who could have done it. Take away my father-in-law's capital and his "knack", and I'd never have got off the ground.

But I wasn't entirely comfortable with this arrangement. I felt I was taking a dishonest short cut, using unfair means to get to where I was. After all, I was part of the late Sixties, early Seventies generation that spawned the radical student movement. We were the first to yell a resounding "No!" at the logic of late capitalism, which had devoured any remaining post-war ideals. It was like the outbreak of a fever just as the country stood at a crucial turning point. And here I was myself, swallowed up by the very same capitalist logic, savouring Schubert's "Winterreise" as I lounged in my BMW, waiting for the lights to change at a crossroads in ritzy Aoyama. I was living someone else's life, not my own. How much of this person I called myself was actually me? And how much was not? These hands clutching the steering wheel – what percentage of them could I call my own? The scenery outside – how much of it was real? The more I thought about it, the less I seemed to understand.

Not that I was unhappy. I had no complaints. Yukiko was a gentle, considerate woman and I loved her. When she gained a bit of weight after giving birth, she started dieting and exercising seriously. A little weight didn't bother me, though – I still thought she was beautiful. I loved to be with her, and I loved sleeping with her. Something about her soothed me. No matter what, I'd be damned if I'd ever return to the kind of life I had in my twenties – days of loneliness and isolation. This was where I belonged. Here was where I was loved and protected. And where I could love and protect others – my wife and my children – back. Being in this position was an unexpected discovery, a totally new experience.

Every morning, I drove my older daughter to her private nursery school, the two of us singing along to a tape of children's songs on the car stereo. Then, before heading out to the small office I rented nearby, I'd play for a while with my younger daughter. In the summer, we'd spend weekends at our cottage in Hakone, watching the fireworks, boating around the lake and strolling in the hills.

When my wife was pregnant I'd had a few flings, but nothing serious. I never slept with any one woman more than once or twice. OK, three times at the most. I never felt I was having an affair with a capital *A*. I just wanted someone to sleep with, the same as my partners. Avoiding entanglements, I chose my bedfellows with care. Maybe I was testing something by sleeping with them. Trying to see what I could find in them, and what they could find in me.

Shortly after our first child was born, a postcard was forwarded to me from my parents' home. It was a card for a funeral, with a woman's name on it. She'd died when she was thirty-six. But I couldn't place the name. The card was postmarked Nagoya. I didn't know a soul there. After a while, though, I realized who the woman was: Izumi's cousin who used to live in Kyoto. I'd completely forgotten her name. Her parents' home, it turned out, was in Nagoya.

It didn't take much to work out that Izumi herself had sent the card to me. No one else would have. At first, though, the reason why was a mystery. But after reading it several times, I could sense the unforgiving coldness that had gone into it. Izumi had never forgotten what I had done, and had never forgiven me. She must have been living a miserable life – a contented woman would never have sent that card. Or if she had, she would have written a word or two of explanation.

The cousin and everything about her came rushing back to me. Her room, her body, the passionate sex we had shared. But the total clarity these memories once had for me was gone, like smoke blown away on the wind. I couldn't imagine why she had died. Thirty-six was such an unnatural age. Her last name was the same as before, which meant she had never married – or had and was divorced.

I found out more about Izumi and her whereabouts from an old high school friend. He'd read a "Tokyo Bar Guide" feature in the magazine *Brutus*, seen my photo, and learned that I was running the two bars in Aoyama. One evening he came over to where I was sitting at the counter and said, *Hi, how's it going?* No implication that he'd gone out of his way to see me. He just happened to be drinking with some of his buddies and came over to say hi.

"I've been to this bar many times," he said. "It's near my office. But I had no idea you were the owner. What a small world."

In high school I was the outsider, but he'd had good marks, played sports and was the type you'd find on the student council. He was a pleasant sort, never pushy. An altogether nice guy. He was in the football team and had been big to begin with, but now he'd put on weight: a double chin, his three-piece suit straining at the seams. *Due to entertaining clients all the time,* he explained. *Big companies are hell on wheels,* he said. *You've got overtime, entertaining clients, job transfers; do a bad job and they kick your butt, meet your quota and they'll raise it. Not the kind of thing decent people should be into.* His office, it turned out, was in Aoyama 1-chome, just down the street.

We talked about the things you'd expect school friends to talk about when they hadn't seen each other for eighteen years – our jobs, marriage, how many children we had, mutual acquaintances we'd run into. That's when he mentioned Izumi.

"There was a girl you were going out with then. You were always together. Something-or-other Ohara."

"Izumi Ohara," I said.

"Right, right," he said. "Izumi Ohara. You know, I ran into her not long ago."

"In Tokyo?" I asked, startled.

"No, not in Tokyo. In Toyohashi."

"Toyohashi?" I said, even more surprised. "You mean Toyohashi in Aichi Prefecture?"

"That's right."

"I don't understand it. Why did you meet Izumi in Toyohashi? What in the world would she be doing there?"

It seemed he caught something hard and unyielding in my voice. "I don't know why," he ventured. "I just saw her there. But there's not much to tell. I'm not even completely sure it was her."

He ordered another Wild Turkey on the rocks. I was drinking a vodka gimlet.

"I don't care if there's not much to tell. I want to know."

"Well . . ." He hesitated. "What I mean is, sometimes I feel like it didn't actually take place. It's a weird feeling, as if I was dreaming but it was real, you know? It's hard to explain."

"But it really did happen, right?" I asked.

"Yes," he said.

"Then tell me."

He gave a nod of resignation and took a sip of his Wild Turkey.

"I went to Toyohashi because my younger sister lives there. I was on a business trip to Nagoya, and it was a Friday, so I decided to go to spend the night at her flat. And that's where I met Izumi. She was in the lift in my sister's block of flats. I was thinking: *Wow, this woman's the spitting image of that Ohara girl.* But then I thought: *No way, it can't be. There's no way I'd meet her in the lift at my sister's, in Toyohashi of all places.* Her face looked different from before. I don't understand, myself, why I soon realized it was her. Instinct, I guess."

"But it was Izumi, right?"

He nodded. "She happened to live on the same floor as my sister. We got off together and walked down the corridor in the same direction. She went into the flat two doors before my sister's. I was curious and checked out the nameplate on her door. Ohara, it said."

"Did she notice you?"

He shook his head. "We were in the same class, but we never really talked to each other. And besides, I've put on over forty pounds since then. She'd never recognize me."

"But was it really Izumi? I wonder. Ohara's a pretty common name. And there must be other people who look like her."

"I was wondering the same thing, so I asked my sister. About what kind of person this Ohara was. My sister showed me the list of tenants' names. You know, those lists they make up when they've got to divide the cost of repainting or something. All the tenants' names were on it. And there it was – Izumi Ohara. With Izumi in katakana, not Chinese characters. There can't be that many with the same combination, surely?"

"Which means she's still single."

"My sister didn't know anything about that," he said. "Izumi Ohara is the block's mystery woman, I found out. No one has ever spoken to her. If you say hello to her as you pass in the corridor, she ignores you. She doesn't answer the bell when you ring. Not exactly about to be voted Most Popular in the Building."

"That can't be her." I laughed and shook my head. "Izumi isn't that kind of person. She was always outgoing, always smiling."

"OK. Maybe you're right. Maybe it was someone else," he said. "Someone with exactly the same name. Let's change the subject."

"But the Izumi Ohara there was living alone?"

"I think so. Nobody's ever seen any men go into her place. Nobody has a clue what she does for a living. It's a complete mystery."

"Well, what do *you* think?"

"About what?"

"About *her*. About this Izumi Ohara who may or may not be someone with the same name. You saw her face in the lift. What did you think? Did she look all right?"

He thought about it. "All right, I suppose," he answered.

"How do you mean, all right?"

He shook his whisky glass; it made a clinking sound. "Naturally, she's aged a bit. She's thirty-six, after all. You and me too. Your metabolism slows down. You put on a few pounds. Can't be a high school student for ever."

"Agreed," I said.

"Why don't we change the subject? It must have been somebody else."

I sighed. Resting both arms on the counter, I looked him straight in the face. "Look, I want to know. I *have* to know.

Just before we left high school, Izumi and I broke up. It was ugly. I screwed up and hurt her a lot. Since then I've never had a way of finding out how she is. I had no idea where she was or what she was doing. So just tell me the unvarnished truth. It was Izumi, wasn't it?"

He nodded. "If you put it that way, yes, it was definitely her. I'm sorry to have to tell you, though."

"So, honestly, how was she?"

He was silent for a while. "First of all, I want you to realize something, OK? I was in the same class as her and thought she was pretty attractive. She was a nice girl. Nice personality, sweet. Not a raving beauty but, you know, appealing. Am I right?"

I nodded.

"You really want me to tell the truth?"

"Go ahead," I said.

"You're not going to like this."

"I don't care. Just tell me the truth."

He took another mouthful of whisky. "I was jealous of you, always together with her. I wanted a girlfriend like that too. Now I can let it all out, I suppose. I never forgot her. Her face was engraved on my memory. That's why, running into her out of the blue in a lift – even eighteen years later – I knew right away. What I'm getting at is this: I have no reason to want to say anything bad about her. It was a shock for me too, you know. I didn't want to admit it was true. Let me put it this way: she's no longer attractive."

I bit my lip. "What do you mean?"

"Most of the children who live in that block of flats are afraid of her."

"Afraid?" I repeated. I looked at him, uncomprehending. He must have chosen the wrong words. "What do you mean – afraid of her?"

"Hey, why don't we stop now? I didn't really want to get into this anyway."

"Wait a second – what does she do? Does she say things to the kids?"

"She doesn't say anything to anybody. As I said before."

"So they are afraid of her face?"

"That's right," he said.

"Does she have a scar or something?"

"No scars."

"Well, then, what are they afraid of?"

He finished his whisky and placed the glass on the counter. And looked at me for a good long time. He appeared flustered and more than a little confused. But something else was in his expression. I could catch a trace of his face as it was back at school. He looked up for a while, staring off into the distance as if watching a stream flowing off and away. Finally he spoke. "I can't explain it well; besides, I don't want to. So don't ask me any more, OK? You'd have to see it with your own eyes to understand. Someone who hasn't actually seen it won't understand anyway."

I nodded, saying nothing more, just sipping at my vodka gimlet. His tone was calm, but any further inquiries I knew he would turn down point-blank.

He started to talk about the two years he had worked in Brazil. *You won't believe it*, he said, *but I ran across someone from my junior high in São Paulo, of all places. Working at Toyota as an engineer.*

His words blew right by me. When he left, he clapped me on the shoulder. "Well, the years change people in many ways, right? I have no idea what went on between you and her before. But whatever it was, it wasn't your fault. To some degree or other, everyone has that kind of experience. Even me. No kidding. I went through the same thing. But there's nothing you can do about it. Another person's life is that person's life. You can't take responsibility. It's as if we're living in a desert. You just have to get used to it. Did you see that Disney film in elementary school – *The Living Desert*?"

"Yes," I answered.

"Our world's exactly the same. Rain falls and the flowers bloom. No rain, they wither up. Bugs are eaten by lizards, lizards are eaten by birds. But in the end every one of them dies. They die and dry up. One generation dies, and the next one takes over. That's how it goes. Lots of different ways to live. And lots of different ways to die. But in the end that doesn't make a bit of difference. *All that remains is a desert.*"

He went home, and I sat alone at the bar, drinking. After the bar was closed for the night, after all the customers had gone, even after the staff had straightened up the place and gone home themselves, I sat there alone. I didn't want to go home right away. I phoned my wife and told her I had something to take care of at work and would be late. I turned out the lights and sat in the dark, drinking whisky. Too much trouble to get ice out, so I drank it straight.

Everyone just keeps on disappearing. Some things just vanish, as if they were cut away. Others fade slowly into the mist. *And all that remains is a desert.*

When I left the bar, just before dawn, a light rain was falling on the main street in Aoyama. I was exhausted. Soundlessly, the rain soaked the rows of tall buildings, standing there like so many gravestones. I left my car in the bar's parking lot and walked home. On the way, I sat down on a handrail and watched a large crow that was cawing from the top of some traffic lights. The four a.m. streets looked shabby and filthy. The shadow of decay and disintegration lurked everywhere, and I was part of it. Like a shadow burned into a wall.

71

8

For ten days or so after the feature article with my name and photo appeared in *Brutus,* old acquaintances dropped into the bar to see me. Junior high and high school friends. Up till then, I'd always wondered who on earth would possibly read all those magazines piled up at the front of every bookshop. But once I myself was featured in one, I discovered that more people than I'd ever imagined were addicted to magazines. In hair salons, banks, coffee shops, trains, every place imaginable, people had magazines open in front of them, as if possessed. Maybe people are afraid they'll have nothing to kill time with, so they just pick up whatever happens to be on hand. It beats me.

Anyway, I can't say it was the most thrilling thing in the world to see these faces from the past. Not that I didn't like talking to them. It put me in a pleasant, nostalgic mood. And they seemed happy to see me. But frankly I couldn't care less about the subjects they brought up. How our old home town had changed, what other school friends were up to now. As if I cared. I was too far removed from that place and time. Besides, everything they talked about brought back memories of Izumi. Every mention of my home town made me picture her alone in that bleak flat. *She's no longer attractive*, my friend had said. *The children are afraid of her.* I couldn't get those two lines out of my head. And the fact that Izumi had never forgiven me.

I'd just wanted to give the bar a little free publicity, but not long after the article came out I began seriously to regret allowing the magazine to report on it. The last thing I wanted was for Izumi to see the article. How would she feel if she saw me, blithely living a happy life, seemingly unscarred by our past?

A month later, though, the cast of old friends had petered out. I suppose that's one point in favour of magazines: you have your moment of fame, then *poof!* you're forgotten. I breathed a sigh of relief. At least Izumi didn't come in. She wasn't a *Brutus* subscriber, after all.

But a couple of weeks after that, after all the hubbub of the article had been forgotten, the last friend showed up.

Shimamoto.

It was the evening of the first Monday in November. And there, at the counter of the Robin's Nest (the name of the jazz club, the title of an old tune I liked), she sat, quietly sipping a daiquiri. I was at the same counter, three seats down, completely oblivious to the fact that it was her. I'd observed that an extremely beautiful woman had come into the bar, but that was all. A new customer; I made a mental note. If I had seen her before, I would have remembered; that's how outstanding she was. Before long, I thought, whoever she was waiting for would show up. Not that women never drank alone in the bar. Some single women seem to expect that men will move in on them; others seem more to be hoping for it. I could always tell which was which. But a woman this beautiful would not be out drinking alone. A woman like this wasn't the type to be thrilled by men making advances. She'd just find it a pain.

That's why I wasn't paying much attention to her. Of course, I studied her when she first came in and glanced at her every so often. She wore just a touch of make-up, and an expensive-looking outfit – a blue silk dress, with a light-beige cashmere cardigan. A cardigan as delicate looking as an onion skin. And on the counter she'd placed a handbag that matched her dress perfectly. I couldn't guess her age. Just the right age was all I could say.

Her beauty took your breath away, but I didn't think she was a film star or a model. Those types did frequent my bar, but you could always tell they were conscious of being on public display, the unbearable *me*ness of being clinging to the air around them. But this woman was different. She was completely relaxed, totally at ease with her surroundings. She rested her chin in her hands on the counter, absorbed in the piano trio's music, all the while sipping her cocktail as if lingering over a particularly well-turned phrase. Every few minutes, she glanced in my direction. I could sense it, physically. Though I was positive she wasn't really looking at me.

I had on my usual outfit – Luciano Soprani suit, Armani shirt and tie. Rossetti shoes. Believe it or not, I wasn't the type to worry about clothes. My basic rule was to spend the bare minimum on them. Outside work, jeans and a sweater were fine. But I did have my own little philosophy of doing business: I wore the kind of clothes I wanted my customers to wear. Doing so, I found, put the staff just that much more on their toes and created the sort of elevated mood I was aiming for. So every time I came to the bar, I made absolutely sure I was wearing a nice suit and tie.

There I sat, then, checking that the cocktails were mixed correctly, keeping an eye on the customers and listening to the piano trio. At first the bar was fairly full, but after nine it started raining and the number of customers tailed off. By ten only a handful of tables were occupied. But the woman at the counter was still there, alone with her daiquiris. I started to wonder about her more. Maybe she wasn't waiting for someone, after all. Not once did she glance at her watch or at the entrance.

Finally she picked up her bag and stepped down from her stool. It was nearly eleven. If you wanted to take the underground home, now was the time to go. Slowly, ever so casually, though, she made her way over to me and sat on the adjacent stool. I caught a faint whiff of perfume. Settling down on the stool, she took a packet of Salems from her bag and put one in her mouth. I caught all this out of the corner of my eye.

"What a lovely bar," she said to me.

I looked up from the book I'd been reading and looked at her uncomprehendingly. Just then something hit me – hard. As if the air suddenly lay heavily on my chest.

"Thanks," I said. She must have known I was the owner. "I'm happy you like it."

"I do, very much." She looked deep into my eyes and smiled. A wonderful smile. Her lips spread wide and small, fetching lines formed at the corners of her eyes. Her smile stirred deep memories – but of what?

"I like your music too." She pointed to the piano trio. "Do you have a light?" she asked.

I had neither matches nor a lighter. I called to the bartender to bring over a book of the bar's matches. And I lit her cigarette for her.

"Thanks," she said.

I looked at her straight on. And I finally understood.

"Shimamoto," I rasped.

"It took you long enough," she said after a while, a funny look in her eyes. "I thought maybe you'd never notice."

I sat there speechless, staring at her as though I were in the presence of some high-tech precision machinery I'd only heard rumours about. It was indeed Shimamoto in front of me. But I couldn't yet grasp the reality of it. I'd been thinking of her for so very, very long. And I was sure I'd never see her again.

"I love your suit," she said. "It's quite becoming."

I nodded wordlessly. The words just wouldn't flow.

"Know something, Hajime? You're much handsomer than you used to be. And a lot better built."

"I swim a lot," I finally managed to say. "I started in junior high and I've been swimming ever since."

"Swimming looks so much fun. I've always thought so."

"It is. But if you practise, anyone can learn, you know," I said. As soon as the words left my mouth, I remembered her leg. *What the hell are you talking about?* I asked myself. I was flustered, fumbling for the right thing to say. But the words eluded me. I rummaged around in my suit pockets for a packet of cigarettes. And then remembered. I'd given up smoking five years before.

Shimamoto watched me silently. She raised her hand and ordered another daiquiri, giving the biggest smile. A truly beautiful smile. The kind of smile that made you want to wrap up the whole picture for safe keeping.

"You still like blue, I see," I said.

"Yes. I always have. You have a good memory."

"I remember almost everything about you: the way you sharpen your pencils, the number of lumps of sugar you put in your tea."

"And how many would that be?"

"Two."

She narrowed her eyes a bit and looked at me.

"Tell me something, Hajime," she began. "That time about eight years ago – why did you follow me?"

I sighed. "I couldn't tell if it was you or not. The way you walked was exactly the same. But there was also something about it that didn't seem like you. I tailed you because I wasn't sure. Tailed isn't the right word. I was just looking for the right moment to talk to you."

"Then why didn't you? Why didn't you just come right out and see if it was me? That would have been faster."

"I don't know," I answered. "Something held me back. My voice just wouldn't work."

She bit her lip a little. "I didn't notice then that it was you. All I could think was that someone was following me and I was afraid. Really. I was terrified. But once I got into the taxi and had a chance to calm down, it came to me. Could that have been Hajime?"

"Shimamoto-san, I was given something then. I don't know what relationship you have to that person, but he gave me – "

She put her index finger to her lips. And lightly shook her head. *Let's not talk about that, all right?* she seemed to be saying. *Please, don't ever bring it up again.*

"You're married?" she asked, changing the subject.

"With two children," I replied. "Both girls. They're still little."

"That's lovely. I think daughters suit you. I can't explain why, but they do."

"I wonder."

"Yes – *somehow.*" She smiled. "But at least you didn't have an only child."

77

"Not that I planned it. It just turned out that way."

"What does it feel like? I wonder. To have two daughters."

"Frankly, a little strange. More than half the children in my older girl's nursery school are only children. The world's changed since we were young. In the city, only children have become more the rule, not the exception."

"You and I were born too soon."

"Maybe," I said. "Perhaps the world's drawing closer to us. Sometimes when I see the two of them playing together at home, I'm amazed. A whole other way of raising children. When I was a child, I always played alone. I thought that was how everyone played."

The piano trio wound up its version of "Corcovado", and the customers applauded. As always, as the night wore on, the trio's playing grew warmer, more intimate. Between numbers the pianist drank red wine, while the bass player smoked.

Shimamoto sipped her cocktail. "You know, Hajime, I wasn't at all sure at first whether I should come here. I agonized over it for nearly a month. I found out about your bar in some magazine I was leafing through. I thought it must be a mistake. You of all people running a bar! But there was your name, and your photograph. Good old Hajime from the old neighbourhood. I was happy to see you again, even if it was in a photograph. But I wasn't sure if meeting you in person was a good idea. Maybe it was better for both of us if we didn't. Maybe it was enough knowing you were happy and doing well."

I listened to her in silence.

"But since I knew where you were, it seemed like a waste not to at least come see you once, so here I am. I sat down over there and watched you. If he doesn't notice me, I thought, maybe I'll just leave without saying anything. But I couldn't stand it. It brought back so many memories and I had to say hello."

"Why?" I asked. "I mean, why did you think it was better not to meet me?"

Tracing the rim of her cocktail glass with her finger, she was lost in thought. "I thought if I met you you'd want to know all about me. Whether I was married, where I lived, what I'd been up to, those kinds of things. Am I right?"

"Well, I'm sure those things would come up."

"Of course."

"But you'd rather not talk about them?"

She smiled perplexedly and nodded. She had a million different variations on a smile. "That's right. I don't want to talk about those things. Please don't ask me why. I just don't want to talk about myself. I know it's unnatural, that it seems as if I'm putting on airs, trying to be a mysterious lady of the night or something. That's why I thought maybe I shouldn't see you. I didn't want you to think I was some strange, conceited woman. That's one reason I didn't want to come here."

"And the other?"

"I didn't want to be disappointed."

I looked at the glass in her hand. I looked at her straight, shoulder-length hair and at her nicely formed thin lips. And at her endlessly deep dark eyes. A small line just above her eyelids caused her to look thoughtful. That line made me imagine a far-off horizon.

"I used to like you very much, so I didn't want to meet you just to be disappointed."

"Have I disappointed you?"

She shook her head slightly. "I was watching you from over there. At first you looked like somebody else. You were so much bigger with a suit on. But when I looked closer, I could make out the Hajime I used to know. Do you realize that your movements have hardly changed since you were twelve?"

"I didn't know that." I tried to smile but couldn't.

"The way you move your hands, your eyes, the way you're always tapping something with your fingertips, the way you knit your eyebrows as if you're displeased about something – they haven't changed a bit. Underneath the Armani suit it's the same old Hajime."

"Not Armani," I corrected her. "The shirt and tie are, but the suit's not."

She smiled at me.

"Shimamoto-san," I began. "You know, I have wanted to see you for a very long time. To talk to you. I had so many things I wanted to tell you."

"I wanted to see you too," she said. "But you never came. You realize that, don't you? After you went off to junior high in another town, I waited for you. Why didn't you come? I was really sad. I thought you'd made new friends in your new home and had forgotten all about me."

Shimamoto crushed out her cigarette in the ashtray. She had clear lacquer on her nails. They were like some exquisitely made handicraft, shiny but understated.

"I was afraid, that's why," I said.

"Afraid?" she asked. "Afraid of what? Of me?"

"No. Not of you. I was afraid of rejection. I was still a child. I couldn't imagine that you were actually waiting for me. I was terrified you would reject me. That I would come to your house to see you and you couldn't be bothered. So I stopped coming. If I was going to get hurt, I thought it would be better to go on living with the happy memories of when we were together."

She tilted her head slightly and rolled a cashew nut in her hand. "Things don't work out easily, do they?"

"No, they don't."

"But we were meant to be friends for a much longer time. I

went all the way through junior high, high school, even college, without making a friend. I was always alone. I imagined how wonderful it would be to have you by my side. If you couldn't actually be there, at least we could write to each other. Things would have been a lot different. I could have stood up to life better." She was silent for a time. "I don't know why, exactly, but after I entered junior high, school life went downhill. And that made me close in on myself even more. A vicious circle, you could call it."

I nodded.

"Up to elementary school I was all right, but after that it was awful. It was as if I was stuck inside a well."

I knew the feeling. That was just how I felt about the eight years of my life between college and marrying Yukiko. One thing goes wrong, then the whole house of cards collapses. And there's no way you can extricate yourself. Until someone comes along to drag you out.

"I had this bad leg and couldn't do what other people do. I just read books and kept to myself. And I stand out. My looks, I mean. So most people ended up thinking I'm a twisted, arrogant woman. And maybe that's who I became."

"Well, you *are* stunning," I said. She put another cigarette between her lips. I struck a match and lit it.

"You really think I'm pretty?" she asked.

"Yes. But you must hear that all the time."

Shimamoto smiled. "Not really. Actually, I'm not that keen on my face. So I'm very happy you said that. Unfortunately, other women don't like me much. Many's the time I thought this: *I don't want people to say I'm pretty. I just want to be an ordinary girl and make friends like everyone else.*"

She reached out a hand and lightly brushed mine on the bar top. "But I'm happy that you're enjoying life."

I was silent.

81

"You are happy, aren't you?" she asked.

"I don't know. At least I'm not unhappy, and I'm not lonely." A moment later I added, "But sometimes the thought strikes me that the happiest time of my life was when we were together in your living room, listening to music."

"You know, I still have those records. Nat King Cole, Bing Crosby, Rossini, the *Peer Gynt* Suite, and all the others. Every single one. A keepsake from my father when he died. I take good care of them, so even now they don't have a single scratch. And you remember how carefully I looked after records."

"So your father died."

"Five years ago, cancer of the colon. A horrible way to go. And he'd always been so healthy."

I'd met her father a few times. He had struck me as being as tough as the oak tree that grew in their garden.

"Is your mother well?" I asked.

"Hmm. I guess so."

Her tone of voice bothered me. "You don't get on with her, then?"

Shimamoto finished her daiquiri, put the glass down and called the bartender over. "Do you have any special house cocktail you'd recommend?"

"We have several original cocktails," I said. "The most popular one's Robin's Nest, after the bar. A little thing I whipped up myself. You use rum and vodka as a base. It's easy going down, but it packs a punch."

"Sounds good for wooing women."

"Well, I thought that was the whole point of cocktails."

She smiled. "OK, I'll try one."

When the cocktail was placed in front of her, she gazed at the colour, then took a tentative sip. She closed her eyes and let the flavour take over. "It's a very subtle taste, isn't it," she said. "Not exactly sweet or tart. Light and simple, but with some body. I had no idea you were so talented."

"I can't build a simple shelf. I have no idea how to change an oil filter on a car. I can't even stick a stamp on an envelope straight. And I'm always dialling the wrong number. But I have come up with a few original cocktails that people seem to like."

She rested her glass on a coaster and looked at it for a while. When she tipped the glass, the reflection of the overhead lights shivered slightly.

"I haven't seen my mother for a long time. We had a row about ten years ago and I've barely seen her since. Of course, we did see each other at my father's funeral."

The piano trio finished an original blues number and began the intro to "Star-Crossed Lovers". When I was in the bar, the pianist would often strike up that ballad, knowing it was a favourite of mine. It wasn't one of Ellington's best-known tunes, and I had no particular memories associated with it; I had just heard it once, and it had struck a chord in me. From college to those bleak publishing years, in the evening I'd listen to the *Such Sweet Thunder* album and the "Star-Crossed Lovers" track over and over again. Johnny Hodges had this sensitive and elegant solo on it. Whenever I heard that languid, beautiful melody, those days came back to me. It wasn't what I'd characterize as a happy part of my life, living as I was, a balled-up mass of unfulfilled desires. I was much younger, much hungrier, much more alone. But I was myself, pared down to the essentials. I could feel each single note of music, each line I read, seep down deep inside me. My nerves were as sharp as a blade, my eyes shining with a piercing light. And every time I heard that music, I recalled my eyes then, glaring back at me from a mirror.

"You know," I said, "once, when I was in the last year of

junior high, I did go to see you. I felt so lonely I couldn't stand it any longer. I tried calling you, but there was no answer. I caught the train over to your place, but someone else's name was on the doorbell."

"My father was transferred and we moved two years after you did. To Fujisawa, near Enoshima. And that's where we stayed until I went to college. I sent you a postcard with our new address on it. Didn't you get it?"

I shook my head. "If I had, I would have written back. Strange, though. There must have been some slip-up somewhere along the line."

"Or maybe we're just unlucky," she said. "Lots of slip-ups and we end up missing each other. But anyway, I want to hear about *you*. What kind of life you've had."

"It'll bore you to tears," I said.

"I don't care. I still want to hear it."

So I gave her a general outline of my life. How I'd had a girlfriend in high school but ended up hurting her badly. I spared her the gory details. I explained how something had happened and I had hurt this girl. And in the process ended up hurting myself. How I went to college in Tokyo and worked at an educational publisher's. How my twenties were filled with friendless, lonely days. I went out with women but was never happy. How from the time I left high school until I met Yukiko and got married, I had never really liked anyone. How I had thought of her often then, thought how wonderful it would be if we could see each other, even for an hour, and talk. Shimamoto smiled.

"You thought about me?"

"All the time."

"I thought about you too," she said. "Whenever I felt bad. You were the only friend I've ever had, Hajime." Her chin resting in one hand propped up on the bar, she closed her

84

eyes as if all the strength had been drained from her body. She didn't wear any rings. The down on her arms trembled. At last she opened her eyes slowly and looked at her watch. I looked at it too. It was nearly midnight.

She picked up her handbag and slipped off the stool. "Goodnight. I'm happy I could see you."

I saw her to the door. "Shall I call you a taxi? It's raining, so it might be hard to find one. If you're thinking of going home by taxi, that is."

Shimamoto shook her head. "It's all right. Don't go to any trouble. I can take care of myself."

"You really weren't disappointed?" I asked.

"In you?"

"Yes."

"No, I wasn't." She smiled. "Rest easy. But that suit – it *is* an Armani, isn't it?"

She wasn't dragging her leg the way she used to. She didn't move very quickly, and if you looked closely, there was something artificial about how she walked, although overall it looked perfectly natural.

"I had an operation four years ago," she said almost apologetically. "I wouldn't say it's a hundred per cent, but it's not as bad as it used to be. It was a big operation, with a lot of scraping of bones, patching them together. But things went well."

"That's great. Your leg looks fine now," I said.

"It is," she said. "Probably it was a good decision. Though maybe I waited too long."

I got her coat from the cloakroom and helped her into it. Standing next to me, she wasn't very tall. It seemed strange. When we were twelve, we were about the same height.

"Shimamoto-san. Will I see you again?"

"Probably," she replied. A smile played around her mouth.

A smile like a small wisp of smoke drifting quietly skyward on a windless day. "Probably."

She opened the door and went out. Five minutes later, I went up the stairs to the street. I was worried she'd have trouble finding a taxi. It was still raining. And Shimamoto was nowhere to be seen. The street was deserted. The headlights of passing cars blurred the wet pavement.

Maybe it was an illusion, I thought. I stood there a long time, gazing at the rainswept streets. Once again I was a twelve-year-old boy staring for hours at the rain. Look at the rain long enough, with no thoughts in your head, and you gradually feel your body falling loose, shaking free the world's reality. Rain has the power to hypnotize.

But this had been no mirage. When I went back into the bar, a glass and an ashtray remained where she had been. A couple of lightly crushed cigarette butts lay in the ashtray, a faint trace of lipstick on each. I sat down and closed my eyes. Echoes of music faded away, leaving me alone. In that gentle darkness, the rain continued to fall without a sound.

9

I didn't see Shimamoto for a long time after that. Every evening, I sat at the counter of the Robin's Nest, passing the time. I read books, glancing every once in a while at the front door. But she didn't come. I was afraid I'd said something wrong, something I shouldn't have, which had upset her. One by one, I reviewed every word we'd spoken that night. But I couldn't come up with anything. Maybe Shimamoto *was* disappointed. A distinct possibility. She was so beautiful and her leg was fixed. What in the world would a woman like that find in me?

The year drew to a close, Christmas came and went, as did New Year. My thirty-seventh birthday rolled around. And January was suddenly over. I gave up waiting for her and only rarely put in an appearance at the Robin's Nest. Being there reminded me of her, causing me to search the faces of the customers in vain. I sat at the bar of my other place, flipping through the pages of books, lost in aimless musings.

For the life of me, I couldn't concentrate.

She'd told me I was the only friend she'd ever had. That made me happy and gave birth to the hope that we might be friends again. I wanted to talk to her about so many things, ask her opinion. If she didn't want to say a thing about herself, I didn't mind. Just to be able to see her, to talk to her, was enough.

But she didn't come. Maybe she was too busy to find the time to see me, I mused. But three months was far too long a gap. Even if she couldn't come to see me, she could at least pick up the phone and call. She'd forgotten all about me, I decided. I wasn't important to her, after all. That hurt, as if a small hole had opened up in my heart. She never should have said that she might come again. Promises – even vague ones like that – linger in your mind.

But in early February, again on a rainy night, she appeared. It was a quiet, freezing rain. Something had come up and I was at the Robin's Nest earlier than usual. The customers' umbrellas carried with them the scent of the chilly rain. A tenor saxophonist had joined the usual piano trio to play a few numbers. He was pretty well known and a stir ran through the crowd. As always, I sat on my corner stool at the bar, reading. Shimamoto sat down quietly beside me.

"Good evening," she said.

I put down my book and looked at her. I couldn't quite believe my eyes.

"I was sure you weren't ever coming here again."

"Forgive me," she said. "Are you angry?"

"I'm not angry. I don't get angry about things like that. This is a bar, after all. People come when they want to, leave when they feel like it. My job's just to wait for them."

"Well, anyway, I'm sorry. I can't explain it, but I just couldn't come."

"Busy?"

"No, not busy," she replied quietly. "I just couldn't come here."

Her hair was wet from the rain. A couple of strands were pasted to her forehead. I asked the waiter to bring her a towel.

"Thanks," she said, and dried her hair. She took out a cigarette and lit it with her lighter. Her fingers, wet and chilled from the rain, trembled slightly.

"It was only drizzling, and I thought I'd catch a taxi, so I just wore a raincoat. But I started walking and ended up walking a long way."

"How about something hot to drink?" I asked.

She looked deep into my eyes and smiled. "Thanks. I'm all right."

In an instant that smile made me forget the three months.

"What are you reading?" She pointed to my book.

I showed it to her. A history of the Sino-Vietnam border conflict after the Vietnam War. She flipped through it and handed it back.

"You don't read novels any more?"

"I do. But not as many as I used to. I don't know anything about new novels. I only like old ones, mostly from the nineteenth century. Ones I've read before."

"What's wrong with new novels?"

"I think I'm afraid of being disappointed. Reading trashy novels makes me feel I'm wasting time. It wasn't always that way. I used to have lots of time, so even though I knew they were junk, I still felt something good would come from reading them. Now it's different. I must be getting old."

"Yes, well, it is true you're getting older," she said, and gave an impish smile.

"What about you? Do you still read a lot?" I asked.

"Yes, all the time. New books, old books. Novels and

everything else. Trashy books, good books. I'm probably the opposite of you – I don't mind reading to kill time."

She asked the bartender to make her a Robin's Nest. I ordered the same. She took a sip of her drink, nodded slightly, and put the glass down on the bar.

"Hajime, why are the cocktails here always so much better than anywhere else?"

"Because we do our best to make them that way," I replied. "No effort, no result."

"What kind of effort do you mean?"

"Take him, for instance," I said, indicating the handsome young bartender, who, all serious concentration, was busy breaking up a chunk of ice with an ice pick. "I pay him a lot of money. Which is a secret as far as the other employees are concerned. The reason for the high salary is his talent for mixing great drinks. Most people don't realize it, but good cocktails demand talent. Anyone can make passable drinks with a little effort. Train them for a few months and they can make a standard-issue mixed drink – the kind most bars serve. But if you want to take it to the next level, you've got to have a special flair. Like playing the piano, painting, running the hundred-metre sprint. Take me: I think I can mix a pretty good cocktail. I've studied and practised. But there's no way I can compete with him. I put in exactly the same alcohol, shake the shaker for exactly the same amount of time and it doesn't taste as good. I have no idea why. All I can call it is talent. It's like art. There's a line only certain people can cross. So once you find someone with talent, you'd best take good care of them and never let them go. Not to mention paying them well." The bartender was gay, so sometimes other gay men gathered at the bar. They were a quiet bunch and it didn't bother me. I really liked the young bartender and he trusted me and worked hard.

"Maybe you have more talent for running a business than would appear," Shimamoto said.

"I'm afraid I don't," I said. "I don't really consider myself a businessman. I just happen to own two small bars. And I don't plan to open any more, or to earn much more than I do at the moment. You can't call what I do talent. But you know, sometimes I imagine things, pretend I'm a customer. If I were a customer, what kind of bar I'd go to, what kind of things I'd like to eat and drink. If I were a bachelor in my twenties, what kind of place would I take a girl to? How much could I spend? Where would I live and how late could I stay out? All sorts of scenarios. The more scenarios I come up with, the more focused my image of the bar becomes."

Shimamoto had on a light-blue turtleneck sweater and a navy-blue skirt. Small earrings glittered at her ears. Her tight-fitting sweater revealed the shape of her breasts. I suddenly found it hard to breathe.

"Go on," she said. Once again that happy smile came to her lips.

"About what?"

"Your business philosophy," she said. "I love to hear you talk like that."

I blushed a little, something I hadn't done in a long while. "I wouldn't call it a business philosophy. You know, this whole process is one I've been doing since I was little: thinking about all kinds of things, letting my imagination take over. Constructing an imaginary place in my head and little by little adding details to it. Changing this and that to suit me. As I told you, after college I worked for a long time for an educational publisher. The work was a complete bore. Absolutely no room for using your imagination. I was sick of it. I couldn't stand going to work any more. I felt as if I was choking, as if every day I was shrinking and one day I would disappear completely."

I took a sip of my drink and glanced around the bar. A nice crowd, considering the rain. The tenor sax player was putting his instrument in its case. I called the waiter over and told him to take a bottle of whisky to the saxophonist, ask him if he'd like something to eat.

"But here it's different," I continued. "You have to use your imagination to survive. And you can put your ideas into practice immediately. No meetings, no executives. No precedents to worry about or Department of Education directives to contend with. Believe me, it's great. Have you ever worked in a company?"

She smiled and shook her head. "No."

"Consider yourself lucky. Me and companies don't get along. I don't think you'd find it any different. Eight years working there convinced me. Eight years down the pan. My twenties – the best years of all. Sometimes I wonder how I put up with it for so long. I suppose that's what I had to go through, though, to get to where I am today. Now I love my job. You know, sometimes my bars feel like imaginary places I created in my mind. Castles in the air. I plant some flowers here, construct a fountain there, crafting everything with great care. People come in, have drinks, listen to music, talk and go home. They are willing to spend a lot of money to come all this way to have some drinks – and do you know why? Because everyone's seeking the same thing: an imaginary place, their own castle in the air, and their very own special corner of it."

Shimamoto took a Salem out of her small handbag. Before she could take out her lighter, I struck a match and lit it for her. I liked to light her cigarettes and watch her eyes narrow as she stared at the flickering flame.

"I haven't worked for one single day in my whole life," she said.

"Not even once?"

"Not even once. Not even a part-time job. Work is totally alien to me. That's why I envy you. I'm always alone, reading books. And any thoughts that happen to occur to me have to do with spending money, not making it." She stretched both arms out in front of me. On her right arm she wore two thin gold bracelets, on her left arm an expensive-looking gold watch. She kept her arms in front of me for a long while, as if they were displaying goods for sale. I took her right hand in mine and gazed for a time at the gold bracelets. I recalled her holding my hand when I was twelve. I could remember exactly how it felt. And how it had thrilled me.

"I don't know ... maybe thinking about ways to spend money is best, after all," I said. I let go of her hand and felt that I was about to drift away somewhere. "When you're always scheming about ways to make money, it's like a part of you is lost."

"But you don't know how empty it feels not to be able to create anything."

"I'm sure you've created more things than you realize."

"What sort of things?"

"Things you can't see," I replied. I examined my hands, resting on my knees.

She held her glass and looked at me for a long while. "You mean like feelings?"

"Yes," I said. "Everything disappears some day. Like this bar – it won't go on for ever. People's tastes change, and a minor fluctuation in the economy is all it would take for this to go under. I've seen it happen; it doesn't take much. Things that have form will all disappear. But certain feelings stay with us for ever."

"But you know, Hajime, some feelings cause us pain *because* they remain. Don't you think so?"

The tenor saxophonist came over to thank me for the

whisky. I complimented him on his performance.

"Jazz musicians these days are so polite," I explained to Shimamoto. "When I was at university, that wasn't the case. They all took drugs and at least half of them were deadbeats. But sometimes you would hear a performance that would blow you away. I was always listening to jazz at clubs in Shinjuku. Always looking to be blown away."

"You like those kinds of people, don't you?"

"I suppose so," I said. "People want to be bowled over by something special. Nine times out of ten you can forget, but that tenth time, that peak experience, is what people want. That's what can move the world. That's art."

I looked again at my hands, resting on my knees. Then I looked up at her. She was waiting for me to continue.

"Anyway, things are different now. I'm the manager of a bar and my job is to invest capital and show a profit. I'm not an artist or someone who creates things. I'm not even a patron of the arts. Like it or not, this isn't the place to look for art. And it's much easier for the manager to have a neatly turned out, polite group than a herd of Charlie Parkers!"

She ordered another cocktail. And lit another cigarette. We were silent for a long while. She seemed lost in thought. I listened to the bass player's long solo in "Embraceable You". The pianist added the occasional accompanying chord, while the drummer wiped away his sweat and had a drink. A regular came up and we chatted for a while.

"Hajime," Shimamoto said a long time later, "do you know any good rivers? A pretty river in a valley, not too big, one that flows fairly swiftly right into the sea?"

Taken by surprise, I looked at her. "A river?" What was she talking about? Her face was expressionless. She was quiet, as if gazing at some far-away landscape. Maybe it was me who was far away – far from her world, at least, with an unimaginable

94

distance separating us. The thought made me melancholy. There was something in her eyes that evoked sadness.

"Why this river all of a sudden?" I asked.

"It just occurred to me," she answered. "*Do* you know of a river like that?"

When I was a student, I travelled around the country quite a bit with a sleeping bag. So I had seen a few Japanese rivers. But I couldn't think of a river like the one she had described.

"I think there might be a river like that on the Japan Sea coast," I said after a great deal of thought. "I don't remember what it's called. But I'm sure it's in Ishikawa Prefecture. It wouldn't be hard to find. It's probably the closest to what you're looking for."

I remembered the river clearly now. I went there in the autumn when I was in my first or second year at college. The foliage was beautiful, the surrounding mountains looking as though they were dyed in blood. The mountains ran down to the sea, the rush of the water was gorgeous, and sometimes you could hear the cry of deer in the forest. The fish I ate were unbelievably delicious.

"Do you think you could take me there?" Shimamoto asked.

"It's all the way over in Ishikawa," I said in a dry voice. "Enoshima I could see, but we'd have to fly, then drive for at least an hour. And stay overnight. I'm sure you understand that's something I can't do at the moment."

Shimamoto shifted slowly on her stool and turned to face me. "Hajime, I know I shouldn't be asking this favour of you. I know that. Believe me, I realize it's a burden to you. But there's no one else I can ask. I have to go there and I don't want to go alone."

I looked into her eyes. They were like a deep spring in the shade of cliffs, which no breeze could ever reach. Nothing moved there, everything was still. Look closely and you could just begin to make out the scene reflected in the water's surface.

"Forgive me." She smiled, as if all the strength had left her. "Please don't think I came here just to ask you that. I wanted only to see you and talk. I didn't plan to bring this up."

I made a quick mental calculation of the time. "If we left really early in the morning and did a round trip by plane, we should be able to make it back by not too late at night. Of course, it depends how long we spend there."

"I don't think it'll take too long," she said. "Can you really spare the time to fly over there and back with me?"

I thought hard. "I think so. I can't say anything definite yet, but I can probably do it. Call me here tomorrow night, all right? I'll be here at this time. I'll work out a plan by then. What's your schedule?"

"I don't have one. Any time that's fine with you is fine with me."

I nodded.

"I'm really sorry," she said. "Maybe I shouldn't have met you again, after all. I know I'll end up ruining everything."

She left just a little before eleven. I held an umbrella over her and flagged down a taxi. The rain was still falling.

"Goodbye. And thank you," she said.

"Goodbye," I said.

I went back into the bar and returned to the same seat at the counter. Her cocktail glass was still there. As was the ashtray, with several crushed-out Salems. I didn't ask the waiter to take them away. For the longest time, I gazed at the faint colour of lipstick on the glass and on the cigarettes.

Yukiko was waiting up for me when I got home. She'd thrown a cardigan over her pyjamas and was watching a video

96

of *Lawrence of Arabia*. The scene where Lawrence, after all sorts of trials and tribulations, has finally made it across the desert and reached the Suez Canal. She'd already seen the film three times. It's a great film, she told me. I can watch it over and over again. I sat down next to her and drank some wine as we watched the end of the film.

Next Sunday there's a get-together at the swimming club, I told her. One of the members owned a large yacht, which we'd been on several times offshore, fishing and drinking. It was a little too cold to go out in a yacht in February, but my wife knew nothing about boats, so she didn't have any objections. I hardly ever went out on Sundays, and she seemed to think it was good for me to meet people in other fields and be outdoors.

"I'll be leaving really early in the morning. And I'll be back by eight, I think. I'll have dinner at home," I said.

"All right. My sister's coming over that Sunday anyway," she said. "If it isn't too cold, maybe we could take a picnic to Shinjuku Goen. Just us four girls."

"Sounds good," I said.

The next afternoon I went to a travel agency and made plane and rental car reservations. There was a flight arriving back in Tokyo at six-thirty in the evening. It looked like I would be back in time for a late dinner. Then I went to the bar and waited for Shimamoto to ring. She phoned at ten. "I'm a little busy, but I think I can make the time," I told her. "Is next Sunday OK?"

"That's fine with me," she replied.

I told her the flight time and where to meet me at Haneda Airport.

"Thank you so much," she said.

After hanging up, I sat at the bar for a while, with a book. The bustle of customers bothered me, though, and I couldn't concentrate. I went to the cloakroom and washed my face and hands with cold water, stared at my reflection in the mirror. I've lied to Yukiko, I told myself. Of course, I'd lied to her before, when I slept with other women. But I had never felt I was deceiving her. Those were just harmless flings. But this time was wrong. It wasn't that I was planning to sleep with Shimamoto, but even so, it was wrong. For the first time in a long while, I looked deep into my own eyes in the mirror. Those eyes told me nothing about who I was. I laid both hands on the sink and sighed deeply.

10

The river flowed swiftly past cliffs, in places forming small waterfalls, in others coming to a halt in pools whose surface faintly reflected the weak sun. An old iron bridge spanned the river downstream. It was so narrow one car could barely squeeze across. Its darkened, impassive metal frame sank deep into the chilled February silence. The only people who crossed over the bridge were the hotel's guests and employees and the people in charge of caring for the woods. When we walked over, we passed no one going the other way and looking back we saw no one. Shimamoto had on a heavy duffel coat, the collar turned up and a scarf wrapped around her up to her nose. She had on casual clothes, good for walking in the mountains, very different from what she usually wore. Her hair was tied back and she wore a pair of rugged-looking work boots. A green nylon shoulder bag was slung over one shoulder. Dressed like that, she looked just like a school girl. On either bank, hard patches of snow remained.

Two crows squatted on top of the bridge, gazing down at the river below, every once in a while releasing grating, scolding caws. Their shrill calls echoed in the leaf-blanketed woods, crossed the river and rang unpleasantly in our ears.

A narrow, unpaved path continued along the far bank, a terribly silent, deserted path leading who knows where. No houses appeared beside it, only the occasional bare field. Snow-covered furrows inscribed bright white lines across the barren land. Crows were everywhere. As if signalling their comrades down the line of our approach, they let out short, sharp caws as we passed. They stood their ground, not trying to fly away. Close to, I could see their sharp, weapon-like beaks and the vivid colouring of their claws.

"Do we still have time?" Shimamoto asked. "Can we walk a little further?"

I looked at my watch. "We're OK. We should be able to stay here for another hour."

"It's so quiet," she said, looking around slowly. Every time she opened her mouth her hard white breath drifted into the air.

"Is this river what you were looking for?"

She smiled at me. "It's as if you could read my mind," she replied. And reached out with her gloved hand to grasp mine, also in a glove.

"I'm glad," I said. "If we had come all this way and you had said this wasn't the place, then what would we do?"

"Have more confidence in yourself. You'd never make that kind of mistake," she said. "But you know, walking like this, just the two of us, I remember the old days. When we used to walk home together from school."

"Your leg isn't like it was, though."

She grinned at me. "You seem almost disappointed."

"Maybe so." I laughed.

"Really?"

"I'm just kidding. I'm very happy your leg's better. Just a bout of nostalgia, I guess."

"Hajime," she said, "I hope you understand how very grateful I am to you for doing this."

"Don't worry about it," I said. "It's like going on a picnic. Except we caught a plane."

Shimamoto walked on for a while, looking ahead. "But you had to lie to your wife."

"I suppose so," I said.

"And that couldn't have been easy. I'm sure you didn't want to lie to her."

I didn't know how to answer. From the woods nearby, a crow let out another sharp caw.

"I've messed up your life. I know I have," Shimamoto said in a small voice.

"Look, let's stop talking about it," I said. "We've come all this way, so let's talk about something more cheerful."

"Like what?"

"Dressed like that, you look like a school girl."

"Thanks," she said. "I wish I were."

We walked slowly upstream. For a while we proceeded in silence, concentrating on our walking. She couldn't walk very fast but was able to handle a slow, steady pace. She held my hand tightly. The path was frozen solid and our rubber soles hardly made a sound.

Just as she had implied, if only we could have walked this way when we were teenagers, or even in our twenties, how wonderful that would have been! A Sunday afternoon, just the two of us strolling along a river like this . . . I would have been ecstatic. But we were no longer at school. I had a wife and children and a job. And I'd had to lie to my wife in order to be here. I had to drive back to the airport, take the flight that arrived in Tokyo at six-thirty, then hurry back to my home, where my wife would be waiting for me.

Finally Shimamoto stopped, rubbed her gloved hands together and gazed all around. She looked upstream, then downstream. On the opposite shore there was a range of mountains, on the left-hand side a line of bare trees. We were utterly alone. The hot-springs hotel, where we'd had lunch, and the iron bridge lay hidden in the shadow of the mountains. Every once in a while, as if remembering its duty, the sun showed its face through a break in the clouds. All we could hear were the screeches of the crows and the rush of water. Someday, somewhere, I will see this scene, I felt. The opposite of déjà vu – not the feeling that I'd already seen what was around me, but the premonition that I would some day. This premonition reached out its long hand and grabbed my mind tight. I could feel myself in its grip. There at its fingertips was me. Me in the future, grown old. Of course, I couldn't see what I looked like.

"This spot will be all right," she said.

"To do what?" I asked.

She smiled her usual faint smile. "To do what I'm about to do," she replied.

We went down to the riverbank. There was a small pool of water, covered by a thin sheet of ice. On the bottom of the pool several fallen leaves lay still, like the bodies of flat, dead fish. I picked up a round stone and rolled it in my hand. Shimamoto took off her gloves and put them in her coat pocket. She undid her shoulder bag, opened it and removed a small bag made out of a pretty cloth. Inside the bag was an urn. She undid the fastening on the lid and carefully opened the urn. For a while she gazed at what was inside.

I stood beside her, watching, without a word.

Inside the urn were white ashes. Very carefully, so that none would spill out, she poured the ashes on to her left palm. There were barely enough to cover her hand. Ash left after a cremation, I thought. It was a quiet, windless afternoon and the ash didn't stir. Shimamoto returned the empty urn to her bag, stuck her index finger into the ash, put the finger to her mouth and licked it. She looked at me and tried to smile. But she couldn't. Her finger remained near her lips.

As she crouched by the river and scattered the ashes, I stood next to her, watching. In an instant the small amount of ash was carried away. She and I stood on the shore, gazing at the water. She stared at her palm, then finally brushed off the remaining ash and put on her gloves.

"Will it really reach the sea?" she asked.

"I think so," I said. But I wasn't sure. The ocean was a fair distance away. Perhaps the ash would settle somewhere. But even so, some of it would, eventually, reach the sea.

She took a piece of board that lay nearby and began digging in a soft spot of ground. I helped her. When we'd dug a small hole, she buried the urn wrapped in cloth. Crows cawed in the distance, observing our actions from beginning to end. No matter; look if you want to, I thought. We're not doing anything bad. All we did was scatter some burned ash in the river.

"Do you think it will turn to rain?" Shimamoto asked, tapping the tip of her boot on the ground.

I looked at the sky. "I think it'll hold out for a while," I said.

"No, that's not what I mean. What I mean is, will the child's ashes flow to the sea, mix with the seawater, evaporate, form into clouds, and fall as rain?"

I looked up at the sky one more time. And then at the river flowing.

"You never know," I replied.

*

103

We headed in our rental car back to the airport. The weather was deteriorating fast. The sky was covered with heavy clouds, no blue visible. It looked as if it would snow at any minute.

"Those were my baby's ashes. The only baby I ever had," Shimamoto said, as if talking to herself.

I looked at her, then looked ahead. Trucks sprayed up muddy melted snow and I had to turn on the wipers every so often.

"My baby died the day after it was born," she said. "It lived just one day. I held it only a couple of times. It was a beautiful baby. So very soft . . . They didn't know the cause, but it couldn't breathe well. When it died it was already a different colour.".

I couldn't say a thing. I reached out my hand and placed it on hers.

"It was a baby girl. Without a name."

"When was that?"

"This time last year. In February."

"Poor thing," I said.

"I didn't want to bury it anywhere. I couldn't stand the thought of it in some dark place. I wanted to keep it beside me for a while, then let it flow into the sea and turn into rain."

She was silent for a long, long time. I kept on driving, not saying a word. She probably didn't feel like talking, so I thought it might be best to leave her alone. But soon I noticed that something was wrong – her breathing sounded strange, a mechanical rasping. At first I thought it was the car engine, but then I realized the sound was coming from beside me. It was as if she had a hole in her windpipe and air was leaking out each time she took a breath.

Waiting for the lights to change, I looked at her. She was white as a sheet and strangely stiff. She rested her head against the headrest and stared straight ahead. She didn't move a muscle; from time to time she would blink, as if forced to. I drove on for a little while and found a place to stop – the car park of a boarded-up bowling alley. On top of the building, which looked like an aeroplane hangar, stood a hoarding with a gigantic bowling pin on it. Alone in the huge car park, we seemed to be in some wilderness at the edge of civilization.

"Shimamoto-san." I turned to her. "Are you all right?"

She didn't answer. She just sat back against the seat, making that unearthly sound. I put my hand to her cheek. It was as cold as the scenery that surrounded us. Not a trace of warmth. I touched her forehead, but it showed no signs of fever. I felt as if I was choking. Was she dying, right here and now? Her eyes were listless as I looked deep into them. I could see nothing; they were as cold and dark as death.

"Shimamoto-san!" I yelled out, but got no response. Her eyes were unfocused. She might not even be conscious. I had to get her to a hospital and fast. We'd definitely miss our plane, but there was no time to worry about that. Shimamoto might die and there was no way I was going to let that happen.

When I started the car again, though, she was trying to say something. I cut the engine, put my ear to her lips, but couldn't make out her words. They were less like words than wind whistling through a crack in a wall. Straining as hard as she could, she repeated her words again and again. Finally a single word came through. "Medicine."

"You want to take some medicine?" I asked.

She gave a tiny nod, so slight I might not have caught it. But it was all she could manage. I rummaged around in her coat pocket. Purse, handkerchief, key holder with a lot of keys, but no medicine. I opened her shoulder bag. Inside was a small packet with four capsules in it. I showed her them. "Is this it?"

Without moving her eyes, she nodded.

I pushed her seat back, opened her mouth and placed one capsule inside. But her mouth was bone dry and nothing would go down. I searched madly for a vending machine, but there wasn't one. And we had no time to look. The only source of water around was the snow. Thank God there was enough of that. I leaped out of the car, scooped up some clean snow under the eaves of the building and put it in Shimamoto's wool cap. Bit by bit, I placed the snow in my mouth and melted it. It took a while to melt enough and the tip of my tongue turned numb. I opened her mouth and let the water flow from mine into hers. Then I held her nose closed and forced her to swallow. She choked a little, but after I did this a couple of times, she was at last able to swallow the capsule.

I looked at the packet. Nothing was written on it, not the name of the medicine, her name, directions. Strange, I thought, considering that such information is usually provided so you won't take a medicine by mistake, or so other people will know what to do. I replaced the packet in her bag and watched her for a while. I had no idea what kind of medicine it was, or what her symptoms were, but since apparently she carried the medicine around all the time, it must work. For her, at least, this attack was not totally unexpected.

Ten minutes later, some colour began to return to her face. I gently put my cheek to hers; warmth was flowing back. I sighed in relief and made her sit back in her seat. She wasn't going to die, after all. I put my arms around her shoulders and rubbed my cheek against hers. Slowly, ever so slowly, she was returning to the land of the living.

"Hajime," she whispered in a dry voice.

"Shouldn't we go to a hospital? Maybe we should find the nearest casualty department," I asked.

"No, we don't need to," she replied. "I'm fine. If I take my medicine, I'm OK. I'll be back to normal in a few minutes. What we should worry about is whether we're going to catch the plane."

"Don't worry about that, for God's sake. We'll stay here until you feel better."

I wiped her mouth with a handkerchief. She took it in her hand and looked at it. "Are you always this kind to everybody?"

"Not to everybody," I said. "To you I am. I can't be kind to everyone. There are limits to my kindness; even to how kind I can be to you. I wish there weren't; then I could do so much more for you. But I can't."

She turned to look at me.

"Hajime, I didn't do this just so that we'd miss the plane," she said in a small voice.

Startled, I gazed at her. "Of course you didn't! You don't need to say that. You were feeling sick. It can't be helped."

"I'm sorry," she said.

"No need to apologize. You didn't do anything wrong."

"But I've ruined your plans."

I stroked her hair, leaned over and kissed her cheek. I was dying to hold her whole body close to me and feel its warmth. But I couldn't. All I could do was kiss her cheek. It was warm, soft and wet. "There's nothing for you to worry about," I said. "Everything will be fine."

By the time we reached the airport and returned the car, it was well past boarding time. Fortunately, though, our plane was delayed. It was still on the runway; the passengers were waiting in the terminal. We both breathed a sigh of relief. *They're servicing the engine*, the person at the counter told us. *We don't know how long it will take*, he said; *we don't have any more information.* It had started to snow when we reached the airport; now it was really coming down. With all the snow, the flight might very well be cancelled.

"What will you do if you can't get back to Tokyo today?" Shimamoto asked me.

"Don't worry. The plane will take off," I said. Not that I had any proof. The idea that it might very well not take off was depressing me. I'd have to come up with a marvellous excuse. Why the hell was I all the way over in Ishikawa? Enough, I said to myself; let's cross that bridge when we come to it. What I had to worry about now was Shimamoto.

"What about you?" I asked. "What will you do if we can't get back to Tokyo today?"

She shook her head. "I'm fine," she said. "The problem is you. You'll be in hot water."

"Maybe. But never fear – they haven't said the flight is cancelled yet."

"I knew something like this would happen," she said, as if to herself. "When I'm around, nothing good ever happens. You can count on it. If I'm involved, then things go bad. Things are going smoothly, then I step in and *wham!* they fall apart."

I sat on the bench in the airport lounge, thinking about the telephone call I'd have to make to Yukiko if the flight was indeed cancelled. I mulled over possible excuses, but everything I came up with sounded lame. I'd gone out saying I was spending Sunday with my friends from the swimming club, then ended up being snowed in in Ishikawa. There was no way I could explain that. "When I left the house I was suddenly overcome by this strong desire to visit the Japan Sea, so I went to Haneda Airport," I could tell her. Do me a favour. If that was the best I could manage, I might as well shut up. Or better yet, maybe I could try the truth. Before long, I realized with a start that I was actually hoping we would be snowed in and the flight cancelled. Subconsciously, I was hoping my wife would find out about my coming here with Shimamoto. I wanted to put an end to excuses, to lies. More than anything, I wanted to stay exactly where I was, with Shimamoto beside me, and let things take their course.

The plane finally took off, an hour and a half late. Inside the cabin Shimamoto leaned against me and slept. Maybe she just had her eyes closed. I put my arm around her shoulder and held her close. Sometimes it seemed she was crying. She was silent the whole time; the first words we spoke were just before the plane landed.

"Shimamoto-san, are you sure you're all right?"

Nestled next to me, she nodded. "I'm fine. As long as I take the medicine. So don't worry." She leaned her head back against my shoulder. "But don't ask me anything, OK? Why that happened."

"Understood. No questions," I said.

"Thank you very much for today," she said.

"What part of today?"

"For taking me to the river. For giving me water from your mouth. For putting up with me."

I looked at her. Her lips were right in front of me. The lips I had kissed as I gave her water. And once more those lips seemed to be seeking me. Slightly parted, with her beautiful white teeth barely visible. I could still feel her soft tongue, which I'd touched slightly as I gave her water. I found it hard to breathe and I couldn't think. My body burned. She wants me, I thought. And I want her. But somehow I held myself in check. I had to stop right where I was. One more step and there would be no turning back.

I called home from Haneda Airport. It was already half-past

eight. Sorry I'm so late, I told my wife. I couldn't get in touch with you. I'll be back in an hour.

"I waited for a long time. I went ahead and ate dinner. I made stew," she said.

I gave Shimamoto a ride in my BMW, which I'd parked at the airport. "Where should I take you?" I asked.

"You can let me off in Aoyama. I can get back from there by myself," she said.

"Will you be all right?"

She smiled broadly and nodded.

We drove in silence till I turned off the main road at Gaien. I'd put a tape of a Handel organ concerto on, very low. Shimamoto held both hands neatly in her lap and looked out of the window. It was Sunday evening and the cars around us were filled with families returning from a day out. I shifted gears briskly.

"Hajime," Shimamoto said as we approached Aoyama Boulevard. "I was thinking earlier how nice it would have been if the plane hadn't taken off."

I was thinking exactly the same thing, I wanted to tell her. But I said nothing. My mouth was dry and words couldn't come. I merely nodded and reached out for her hand. At the corner of Aoyama 1-chome, she told me to stop the car and I let her out.

"May I come to see you again?" she asked me softly as she opened the door. "You can still stand being around me?"

"I'll be waiting," I said.

Shimamoto nodded.

As I drove away, I thought this: *If I never see her again, I will go insane*. Once she got out of the car and was gone, my world was suddenly hollow and meaningless.

11

Four days after Shimamoto and I returned from Ishikawa, I got an unexpected call from my father-in-law. He said he had a favour to ask and invited me to lunch the next day. I agreed, frankly surprised. Usually his busy schedule allowed only for business lunches.

Six months before, his company had moved from Yoyogi to a new seven-storey building in Yotsuya. His offices occupied the top two floors, and he rented out the lower five to other companies, restaurants and shops. It was the first time I'd been there. Everything glittered, brand spanking new. The lobby had a marble floor, a cathedral ceiling, flowers piled high in a huge ceramic vase. When I got out of the lift at the sixth floor, I was met by a young receptionist with hair so gorgeous she looked as if she belonged in a shampoo commercial. She called my father-in-law to tell him I had arrived. She had a dark-grey high-tech phone that reminded me of a spatula with a calculator attached. She beamed at me and said, "Please go on in. The president is expecting you." A gorgeous smile, though not in the same class as Shimamoto's.

The presidential office was on the top floor and a large picture window gave a view of the city. Not the most heart-warming scene, but the room was bright and spacious. An impressionist painting hung on the wall. A picture of a light-house and a boat. It looked like a Seurat, very possibly an original.

"Business is booming, I take it?" I said.

"It's not bad," he replied. He walked to the window and pointed outside. "Not bad at all. And it's going to get even better. This is the time to make some money. For people in my line of work, a chance like this comes along only once every twenty or thirty years. If you don't make money now, you never will. Do you know why?"

"I have no idea. The construction business isn't exactly my field."

"Look out at Tokyo here. See all the empty plots of land? Like a mouth full of missing teeth. If you look down from above like this, there it is for all the world to see, but walk around town at ground level and you'll miss it. There used to be old houses and buildings in those spaces, but they've been torn down. The price of land has shot up so much that old buildings aren't profitable any more. You can't charge a high rent and it's hard to find tenants. That's why they need newer, bigger buildings. And private homes in the city – well, people can't afford their property taxes or inheritance taxes. So they sell out and move to the suburbs. And professional construction companies buy up the old houses, put 'em to the wrecking ball and construct brand-new, more functional buildings. So before long all those empty spaces will have new buildings on them. In a couple of years you won't recognize Tokyo. There's no shortage of capital. The Japanese economy's booming, stocks are up. And banks are bursting at the seams with cash. If you have land as collateral, the banks will lend you as much as you could possibly want. That's why all these buildings are going up one after another. And guess who builds them? Men like me."

"I see," I said. "But if all those buildings are built, what will happen to Tokyo?"

"What will happen? Well, it'll get more lively, more beautiful, more functional. Cities reflect the way the economy's going, after all."

"That's all very well, but Tokyo's already choked with cars. Any more skyscrapers and the roads will turn into one huge car park. And how's the water supply going to be maintained if there's a dry spell? In the summer, when people all have their air conditioners on, they won't be able to keep up with the demand for electricity. The power plants are run by fuel from the Middle East, right? What happens if there's another oil crisis? Then what?"

"Let the government figure that out. Isn't that what we're paying high taxes for? Let all those Tokyo University graduates rack their brains. They're always running around with their snooty noses in the air – like they're the ones who really run the country. Let them put their pointy heads to work for a change. I don't have the answer. I'm a simple builder. Orders for buildings come in, and I build them. That's what you call market forces, am I right?"

I said nothing. I hadn't come all the way here for a debate on the Japanese economy.

"Anyhow," he said, "let's drop all this complicated stuff and go and eat. I'm starving."

Getting in his huge black Mercedes, we drove to his favourite grilled-eel restaurant, in Akasaka. We were shown to a private room in the back, where we settled in for a meal. It was the middle of the day, so I only sipped a little sake, but my father-in-law threw back one cup after another.

"You said you had something you wanted to talk about?" I asked. If it was bad news, I'd rather get it out of the way first.

"I have a favour to ask," he said. "Nothing really big. I just need to use your name for something."

"My name?"

"I'm starting a new company and I need to use somebody else's name as the founder. You don't need any special qualifications. Just your name. I promise it won't cause you any trouble and I'll make it worth your while."

"Don't worry about that," I said. "If it will help you, you can use my name as many times as you like. But what kind of company are you talking about? If my name's going to be listed as the founder, I might as well know that much."

"Well, to tell you the truth, it's not an actual company," my father-in-law answered. "It's a company in name only, I should say. It doesn't really exist."

"A fake company, in other words. A dummy company."

"I suppose you could say that."

"What's the point? Is it a tax dodge?"

"Hmm . . . not exactly," he said reluctantly.

"Bribes?" I ventured.

"Sort of," he said. "I'll be the first to admit this isn't the greatest thing in the world to be involved in. But in my line of work you have to."

"Well, what if some problem develops?"

"There's nothing illegal about forming a company."

"I'm talking about what that company does."

He took a cigarette out of his pocket and lit it with a match. And exhaled smoke into the air above him.

"There won't be any problems. Even if there were, anybody

with half a brain could see that you just lent your name to it. Your wife's father asked you to let him use your name and you did. No one's going to hold you responsible."

I didn't say anything for a while. "Where are all these bribes going to end up?"

"You're better off not knowing."

"Tell me more about these so-called market forces," I said. "Are they going into some politician's pocket?"

"A little," he said.

"Bureaucrats'?"

My father-in-law stubbed out his cigarette in the ashtray. "That would be graft, wouldn't it. They'd arrest me."

"But everybody in your business does it, right?"

"I suppose," he said. And he made a pained face. "But not to the point where they're arrested."

"What about the yakuza? They're pretty helpful when it comes to buying up land, aren't they?"

"I've never got along with them. Anyhow, I'm not trying to corner the market. It's lucrative, but I don't do it. As I said, I'm just a simple builder."

I sighed deeply.

"I knew you wouldn't like this," he said.

"It doesn't matter if I like it or not, since you've already included me in the equation and gone ahead, right? On the assumption that I'd agree."

"I'm afraid you're right." He laughed weakly.

I sighed again. "Dad, to tell you the truth, I don't like this kind of thing. I don't mean because it's illegal or anything. But I'm just an ordinary guy living an ordinary life. And I'd rather not get involved in backroom deals."

"I'm well aware of that," he said. "So leave it all to me. I won't leave you hanging out to dry. If I did, then Yukiko and the children would be involved too. And I'm not about to let that happen. You know how much my daughter and grand-children mean to me."

I nodded. I couldn't very well refuse his request. It depressed me. Little by little, I would get snared by the world out there. This was the first step; first I say yes to this, then later on it'll be something else.

We ate some more. I drank tea, while my father-in-law put away the sake at an even faster rate.

"How old are you now?" he asked suddenly.

"Thirty-seven," I replied.

He looked at me fixedly.

"Thirty-seven's the age when you play around the most," he said. "Work's going well, your confidence is up. So women come to you, right?"

"In my case, not that many, I'm afraid." I laughed, studying his expression. For a second I panicked, positive that he'd found out about me and Shimamoto and that was why he asked me here today. But he was just making small talk.

"When I was your age I played around quite a bit. So I won't tell you not to have affairs. It's strange for me to be saying this to my daughter's husband, but actually I think a fling or two on the side isn't all bad. It refreshes you. Get it out of your system every once in a while and your home life will improve; you'll be able to concentrate on work too. So if you were to sleep with other women, I for one wouldn't say a word. Playing around's all right by me, but be very careful in choosing your partners. Get involved with the wrong person and your life goes down the pan. I've seen it happen a million times."

I nodded. And suddenly recalled hearing from Yukiko that her brother and his wife weren't getting on together. Her brother, who was a year younger than me, had a girlfriend and didn't come home much any more. I imagined my father-in-law

116

was worried about his oldest son and that was why he had brought all this up.

"Anyhow, don't get involved with some worthless bit of tail. Do that and you'll soon be worthless yourself. Play around with a stupid woman and you'll turn stupid too. Which isn't to say that you should get involved with some high-class woman. That would make it tough to go back to what's waiting for you at home. Do you understand what I'm telling you?"

"I think so," I replied.

"As long as you keep a few things in mind, you'll be all right. First, don't set the woman up with her own place. That's a definite mistake. Second, no matter what, come back home by two a.m. Two a.m. is the point of no return. Finally, don't use your friends as excuses to cover up your affairs. You may be found out. If that happens, well, there's not much you can do about it. But there's no need to lose a friend in the process."

"It sounds like you're speaking from experience."

"You've got it. Man learns from experience alone," he said. "There are some people who don't; I know you're not one of them. You have a very discriminating eye, something only experience can teach you. I've been to your bars just a couple of times, but it's plain to see. You know how to hire good people and how to treat them well."

I was silent, waiting for him to go on.

"You also have a good eye for choosing a wife. Yukiko's very happy living with you. And your children are wonderful kids. I'm grateful to you."

He's pretty drunk, I thought. But I didn't say anything.

"You probably don't know this, but Yukiko tried to commit suicide once. Took an overdose of sleeping pills. We rushed her to the hospital and she didn't regain consciousness for two days. I was sure she wouldn't make it. Her body was cold and she was hardly breathing. She's a goner, I thought. I felt as if the world had collapsed."

I looked up at him. "When did this happen?"

"When she was twenty-two. Right after she graduated from university. It was over a man. A real jerk she'd got engaged to. Yukiko looks really quiet, but underneath she's tough. And clever. That's why I can't figure out why she ever got involved with a man like that." He leaned against the pillar in the traditional-style room we were in, put a cigarette between his lips, and lit it. "Well, that was her very first man. The first time everyone makes mistakes. For Yukiko, though, it was a huge shock. That's why she tried to kill herself. For a long time afterwards she wouldn't have anything to do with men. She'd always been pretty outgoing, but she stopped talking to people and stayed holed up in the house. Once she met you, though, she began to cheer up. She did a complete turn-around. I remember you met each other on a trip?"

"That's right. At Yatsugatake."

"I nearly had to shove her out the door to get her to go. I thought travel might do her good."

I nodded. "I knew nothing about the suicide," I said.

"I thought it was better you didn't, so I never mentioned it. But it's high time you knew. The two of you are going to be together for a long time, so you'd better know everything – the good and the bad. Besides, it happened a while ago." He closed his eyes and blew a puff of smoke into the air. "It's funny for me as her parent to say this, but she's a good woman. I've played around a lot and I have an eye for the ladies. Whether she's my daughter or not, I'm able to judge women pretty well. My younger daughter's much prettier, but Yukiko's the better person. You're a good judge of people."

I was silent.

"You don't have any brothers and sisters, do you?"

"No, I don't," I said.

"Do you think I love all three of my children equally?"

"I have no idea."

"How about you? Do you love both of your daughters the same?"

"Of course."

"That's because they're both still little," he said. "Wait till they grow up. First you'll like this one, but then you'll start leaning towards the other. Some day you'll see what I mean."

"Really?" I said.

"I'd never say this to them, but of my three kids I like Yukiko best. I feel bad for the others when I say this, but there it is. Yukiko and I get along well and I can trust her."

I nodded.

"You have a good eye for people and that's a wonderful talent you've got to cherish. I'm a hopeless case myself, but at least I've helped raise something not quite so hopeless."

I assisted my now thoroughly drunk father-in-law into his Mercedes. He sank back into the rear seat, spread his legs apart and closed his eyes. I hailed a taxi and went home. As soon as I arrived, Yukiko wanted to hear the reason for our lunch.

"Nothing really important," I said. "Your father just wanted to have someone to drink with. He ended up pretty drunk. I wonder that he can go back to work in that condition."

"He's always like that." Yukiko laughed. "He has some drinks at lunch, then takes an hour's nap on the sofa in his office. The company hasn't gone into liquidation yet. Don't you worry about him."

"He doesn't seem to hold his drink like he used to."

"No, he doesn't. Before Mum died, he could drink like a fish and never show it. He was tough. But it can't be helped.

Everybody gets old."

She brewed a pot of coffee and we sat at the dining table, drinking it. I decided not to say anything about the dummy company and her father's request. She'd only think he was bothering me and she wouldn't like it. *It's true you borrowed money from Father, but that has nothing to do with this,* Yukiko would no doubt say. *You're paying it back, with interest, right?* But the situation wasn't quite that simple.

My younger daughter was fast asleep in her room. When I finished my coffee, I enticed Yukiko into bed. We stripped naked and held each other tight there in the glare of the sun. I took my time warming her body up, then entered her. But all the time I was inside her, it was Shimamoto I saw. I closed my eyes and felt I was holding Shimamoto. And I came violently.

I took a shower, then went back to bed to sleep for a while. Yukiko was already dressed, but after I slipped into bed, she got under the covers and put her lips against my back. I lay silent with my eyes closed. I'd had sex with her, all the while thinking of another woman, and the guilt was getting to me.

"You know, I really do love you," Yukiko said.

"We've been married seven years, we have two kids," I said. "About time for you to get tired of me, don't you think?"

"Perhaps. But I still love you."

I held her close. And began to undress her. I pulled off her sweater and skirt, her underwear.

"Whoa! You're not planning what I think you're planning, are you?" she asked in surprise.

"Of course," I said.

"Special-entry time for my diary today," she said.

This time I tried hard not to think of Shimamoto. I held Yukiko's body, looking at her face and concentrating only on her. I kissed her lips, her neck, her breasts. And I came inside her. Afterwards, I held her for a long time.

"Are you all right?" she asked, her eyes on me. "Did something happen today with you and Father?"

"Nothing happened," I replied. "Not a thing. I just feel like staying like this for a while."

"Be my guest," she said. And she held me tight, with me still inside her. I closed my eyes and pulled her hard against my body, as though, if I didn't, I would fly off into the void.

As I held her, I remembered the attempted suicide her father had told me about. *I was sure she wouldn't make it. She's a goner, I thought.* If things had taken even the slightest of wrong turns, I wouldn't be holding her body like this. Gently I touched her shoulder, her hair and breasts. They were real – warm and soft. Beneath my palm I could feel her life. No one could say how long that life would last. Whatever has form can disappear in an instant. Yukiko. This room. These walls, this ceiling, this window. They might all be gone before we knew it. Suddenly Izumi came to mind. That man had hurt Yukiko deeply and I had done the same to Izumi. Yukiko happened to meet me after that, but Izumi was all alone.

I kissed Yukiko's soft neck.

"I'm going to sleep for a while," I said. "And then I'll go to the nursery school to pick her up."

"Sleep well," she told me.

I slept for just a short time. When I opened my eyes, it was after three p.m. From the bedroom window I could see the Aoyama Cemetery. I sat down in a chair by the window and stared at it for a long time. So many things looked different now, now that Shimamoto had shown up in my life again. I could hear Yukiko preparing dinner in the kitchen. The sounds rang hollowly in my ears, like those transmitted down a pipe from a world terribly far away.

I got the BMW out of the underground garage and headed for school to pick up my daughter. They had some special programme that day, so it was almost four when she appeared at the gates. You could always count on a line of shiny, expensive cars there – Saabs, Jaguars, even the occasional Alfa Romeo. Young mothers in expensive-looking coats got out of the cars, collected their children, deposited them in the cars and drove off. My daughter was the only child whose father came to pick her up. When I saw her, I called out her name and waved. She waved her tiny hand and came towards me. Then she saw a little girl sitting in a blue Mercedes 260E and ran over to her, yelling out something. The girl had on a red woollen cap and was leaning out of the car window. The girl's mother wore a red cashmere coat and a large pair of sunglasses. When I went over there and took my daughter's hand, the woman turned to me and smiled broadly. I returned the smile. The red coat and the sunglasses made me think of Shimamoto. The Shimamoto I followed from Shibuya to Aoyama.

"Hi," I said.

"Hi," she said.

The woman was stunning. She couldn't have been much more than twenty-five. Her car stereo was playing the Talking Heads' song "Burning Down the House". On the back seat were two paper carrier bags from Kinokuniya. She had a beautiful smile. My daughter whispered for a while to her little friend, then said goodbye. *'Bye*, said the girl. Then she pushed the button and closed the car window. I took my daughter's hand and we walked over to where the BMW was parked.

"How was your day? Anything good happen?" I asked.

She shook her head emphatically. "Nothing good at all. It was terrible," she said.

"Tough time for both of us," I said. I leaned over and kissed her forehead, and she made the same sour face owners of snobby French restaurants produce when you hand them your American Express card. "I'm sure tomorrow will be better," I told her.

I wanted to believe that too. When I opened my eyes tomorrow, the world would be new, and every problem would be solved. But I couldn't swallow that scenario. For I had a wife and two daughters. And I was in love with someone else.

"Daddy?" my daughter said. "I want to ride a horse. Will you buy me a horse one day?"

"OK. One day," I said.

"When's one day?"

"When Daddy's saved up some money. Then he'll buy you a horse."

"Do you have a piggy bank, Daddy?"

"Yes, a very big one. As big as this car. If I don't save up that much money, I won't be able to buy you a horse."

"If we ask Grandpa, do you think he'll buy me a horse? Grandpa's rich."

"That's right," I said. "Grandpa has a piggy bank as big as that building over there. With lots of money inside. But it's so big it's hard to get the money out."

My daughter thought about it for a while.

"But can I ask Grandpa sometime? To buy me a horse?"

"Of course, you can ask him. Who knows, he might even buy one for you."

We talked about horses all the way home. What colour horse she liked. What name she'd give it. Where she would like to ride to. Where the horse would sleep. I put her in the lift and headed for work. What would tomorrow bring? I wondered. Both hands on the wheel, I closed my eyes. I didn't feel as if I was in my own body; my body was just a lonely, temporary container I happened to be borrowing.

What would become of me tomorrow I did not know. Buying my daughter a horse – the idea took on an unexpected urgency. I had to buy it for her before things disappeared. Before the world fell to pieces.

12

From then until the spring, Shimamoto and I saw each other almost every week. She would stop by one of the bars, more often than not the Robin's Nest, always after nine. She'd sit at the bar, have a couple of cocktails and leave around eleven. I'd sit beside her and we'd talk. I don't know what my employees thought, but I didn't care. It was like when we were at school together and I didn't let what my school friends thought about the two of us concern me.

Occasionally she'd phone to invite me to have lunch. Most often we'd arrange to meet at a café on Omote Sando. We'd have a light meal and then walk. We'd be together for two, at most three, hours. When it was time for her to leave, she'd glance at her watch and then smile at me. "Well, I'd better be going," she'd say. I couldn't read any of the emotions behind that smile. Whether she felt sad or not at leaving, or maybe relieved to be rid of me, I had no idea. I couldn't even tell if she really did have to get home.

Anyhow, during the couple of hours we were together, we hardly stopped talking. Not once, though, did our bodies come in contact. Not once did I put my arm around her shoulder or even so much as hold her hand.

Back on the streets of Tokyo, Shimamoto had her usual cool, attractive smile. No more the rush of violent emotions she had displayed on that cold February day in Ishikawa. The warm closeness born on that day was gone. As if by unspoken agreement, we never mentioned our strange little trip.

As we walked side by side, I wondered what feelings she held in her heart. And where those feelings would lead her. Sometimes I looked deep into her eyes, but all I could detect was a gentle silence. As before, the line of her eyelids brought to mind the horizon, far off in the distance. At long last I could understand Izumi's loneliness when we were going out together. Shimamoto had her own little world within her. A world that was for her alone, one I could not enter. Once, the door to that world had begun to open a crack. But now it was closed.

I felt again like a helpless, confused twelve-year-old. I had no idea what I should do, what I should say. I tried my best to stay calm and use my head. But it was hopeless. Everything I said and did was wrong. Every emotion was swallowed up in that radiant smile. *Don't worry,* her smile told me. *It's all right.*

I was completely in the dark about Shimamoto's life. I didn't even know where she lived. Or who she lived with. Whether she was married, or had been. The only thing I knew was that last February she had had a baby, which died the next day. And that she'd never worked. Still, she always wore the most expensive-looking clothes and accessories, which meant that she had a fair amount of money. That's all I knew about her. She was probably married when she had the baby, but I couldn't be sure. Thousands of babies are born out of wedlock every day, aren't they?

As time passed, Shimamoto began to tell me a little about her junior high school and high school days. There being no direct connection between those days and her present life, she didn't mind talking about them. I discovered how terribly lonely she had been. As she grew up, she had tried her best to be fair to everyone around her, never to make excuses. "Start making excuses and there's no end to it," she told me. "I can't live that kind of life." But things didn't work out well. Her attitude only gave rise to stupid misunderstandings, which hurt her deeply. Steadily, she shut herself away. Waking up in the morning, she'd vomit and refuse to go to school.

She showed me a photograph taken when she started at high school. She was sitting on a chair in a garden, with sunflowers in bloom around her. It was summer, and she had on denim shorts and a white T-shirt. She was gorgeous. Facing the camera, she was smiling broadly. Compared with her smile now, she looked a bit self-conscious. Even so, it was a wonderful smile. The kind of smile that, because of its very precariousness, affected people all the more. Certainly not the smile of a lonely girl spending each day in misery.

"Judging by this picture," I told her, "I'd say you were the happiest girl in the world."

She shook her head slowly. Charming lines appeared at the corners of her eyes; she looked as if she were recalling some far-off scene from the past. "Hajime, you can't tell anything from photographs. They're just a shadow. The real me is far away. That won't show up in a picture."

The photograph brought a pain to my chest. It made me realize what an awful amount of time I had lost. Precious years that could never be recovered, no matter how much I struggled to bring them back. Time that existed only then, only in that place. I gazed at the photo for a very long time.

"What's so interesting about it?" she asked.

"I'm trying to fill in time," I replied. "It's twenty-five years since I saw you last. I want to fill in that gap, even a little."

She smiled and looked at me quizzically, as if there was something weird about my face. "It's strange," she said. "You want to fill in that blank space of time, but I want to keep it all blank."

Throughout junior high and high school, she never had a real boyfriend. She was a beautiful girl, so boys paid attention to her, but she barely noticed them. She went out with a few, but never for very long.

"Boys that age are hard to like. You understand. Teenage boys are uncouth and selfish. And all they can think about is getting their hand up a girl's skirt. I was so disappointed. I wanted what the two of us used to have."

"Yes, but when I was sixteen I wasn't any different – uncouth, selfish, and trying to get my hand up a girl's skirt. That was me in a nutshell."

"I guess it was better I didn't meet you then," she said, and smiled. "Saying goodbye at twelve, meeting again at thirty-seven . . . maybe this is the best way for us, after all."

"I wonder."

"Now you're able to think of a few things other than what's under a girl's skirt, aren't you?"

"A few," I said. "But if you're worried, maybe next time you'd better wear trousers!"

Shimamoto gazed at her hands, resting on the table-top, and laughed. She didn't wear a ring. A bracelet and a new watch every time we met. And earrings. But never a ring.

"I didn't want to be a burden to any boy," she continued. "You know what I mean. There were so many things I couldn't do. Going on picnics, swimming, skiing, skating, dancing at a disco. It was hard enough just to walk. All I could do was sit with someone, talk and listen to music, which boys that age couldn't stand for very long. And I hated that."

She drank Perrier with a twist of lemon. It was a warm afternoon in the middle of March. Some of the young people passing by on the street outside were wearing short-sleeved shirts.

"If I had gone out with you then, I know I would have ended up being a burden to you. You would soon have been fed up with me. You would have wanted to be more active, to take a running leap into the wide world outside. And I wouldn't have been able to endure it."

"Shimamoto-san," I said, "that's impossible. I would never have been impatient with you. We had something very special. I can't explain it in words, but it's true. A special, precious something."

She looked at me closely, her expression unchanged.

"I'm not some great person," I continued. "I'm not much to brag about. I used to be pretty crude, insensitive and arrogant. So maybe I wouldn't have been the right person for you. But there is one thing I am certain about: I never, *ever* would have been bored with you. That, at least, makes me different from other people you knew. In that sense I am indeed a special person for you."

Shimamoto's gaze again shifted to her hands on the table. She lightly spread her fingers, as if checking all ten of them.

"Hajime," she began, "the sad truth is that some things can't go backwards. Once they start going forward, no matter what you do, they can't go back to the way they were. If even one little thing goes awry, then that's how it will stay for ever."

*

129

Once, she phoned to invite me to a concert of Liszt piano concertos. The soloist was a famous South American pianist. I cleared my schedule and went with her to the concert hall at Ueno Park. The performance was brilliant. The soloist's technique was outstanding, the music both delicate and deep and the pianist's heated emotions were there for all to feel. Still, even with my eyes closed, the music didn't sweep me away. A thin curtain stood between myself and the pianist, and no matter how much I might try, I couldn't get to the other side. When I told Shimamoto this after the concert, she agreed.

"But what was wrong with the performance?" she asked. "I thought it was wonderful."

"Don't you remember?" I said. "The record we used to listen to, at the end of the second movement there was this tiny scratch you could hear. *Putchi! Putchi!* Somehow, without that scratch, I can't get into the music!"

Shimamoto laughed. "I wouldn't exactly call that art appreciation."

"This has nothing to do with art. Let a bald vulture eat art up, it wouldn't bother me. I don't care what anybody says; I like that scratch!"

"Maybe you're right," she admitted. "But what's this about a bald vulture? Ordinary vultures I know about – they eat corpses. But bald vultures?"

In the train on the way home, I explained the differences in great detail: the difference in where they are born, their call, their mating periods. "The bald vulture lives by devouring art. The ordinary vulture lives by devouring the corpses of unknown people. They're completely different."

"You are strange!" She laughed. And there in the train seat, ever so slightly, she moved her shoulder to touch mine. The one and only time in the past two months our bodies had touched.

March passed and so did April. My younger daughter started going to nursery school. With the children away from home, Yukiko began doing volunteer work in the community, helping out at a home for handicapped children. Most of the time it was my job to take the kids to school and pick them up again. Whenever I was busy, my wife took over. Watching the children grow, day by day, I could feel myself ageing. All by themselves, regardless of any plans I might have for them, they were getting bigger. I loved my daughters, of course. Watching them grow up made me happier than anything. Sometimes, though, seeing them grow bigger by the month made me feel oppressed. It was as if a tree were growing inside my body, laying down roots, spreading its branches, pushing down on my organs, my muscles, bones and skin, forcing its way outwards. It was so stifling at times that I couldn't sleep.

Once a week I met Shimamoto. And daily I shuttled my daughters back and forth to school. And a couple of times a week I made love to my wife. Since I had started seeing Shimamoto again, I made love to Yukiko more often. Not out of guilt, though. Loving her, and being loved, was the only way I could hold myself together.

"You've changed. What's going on?" Yukiko asked me one afternoon after sex. "Nobody told me that when men reach thirty-seven their sex drive goes into a higher gear."

"Nothing's going on. Same old thing," I replied.

She looked at me for a while. And shook her head slightly. "Sometimes I wonder what's going on inside that head of yours," she said.

In my free time I listened to classical music and gazed out at Aoyama Cemetery. I didn't read as much as I used to. My concentration was shot to pieces.

Several times I saw the young woman in the Mercedes

131

260E. Waiting for our daughters to come out of the school gates, we stood making small talk, the kind of gossip only someone living in Aoyama would comprehend. Advice about which supermarket you could park at easily and when; the latest on a certain Italian restaurant, which had changed chefs and now couldn't serve decent food; news that the Meiji-ya import store was having a sale on imported wine next month, and so on. Damn, I thought. I've become a regular gossipy hausfrau! But these things were all we had in common.

In the middle of April Shimamoto disappeared again. The last time I saw her, we were sitting in the Robin's Nest. Just before ten, a phone call came from my other bar, something I had to take care of right away. "I'll be back in thirty minutes or so," I told her.

"All right," she said, smiling. "I'll read a book while you're gone."

I rushed to deal with the problem, then hurried back, but she was no longer there. It was a little after eleven. On the counter, on the back of a match book, she'd left a message: "Probably I won't be able to come here for a while," the note said. "I have to go home now. Goodbye. Take care."

I was at a loose end for days. I paced around my house, wandered the streets aimlessly and went to pick up my daughters early. And I talked to the Mercedes 260E lady. We went to a nearby café for a cup of coffee, gossiping as usual about the state of the vegetables at the Kinokuniya Market, the fertilized eggs at the Natural House food store, the bargain sales at Miki House. The woman was a fan of Inaba Yoshie's designer wear and before the season arrived she ordered all the clothes she wanted from the catalogue. We talked, too, about the wonderful eel restaurant near the police station on Omote Sando, which was no longer in business.

We enjoyed talking. The woman was more friendly and open than she had appeared to be at first. Not that I was sexually attracted to her. I just needed someone – anyone – to talk to. What I wanted was harmless, meaningless talk, talk that would lead anywhere but back to Shimamoto.

When I ran out of things to do, I'd go shopping. Once, on a whim, I bought six shirts. I bought toys and dolls for my daughters, accessories for Yukiko. I stopped by the BMW showroom a couple of times to check out the M5; I didn't really plan to buy one, but I let the salesman give me his pitch.

A few unsettled weeks like this and I found myself able to concentrate again. I'm going nowhere fast here, I decided. So I phoned a designer and an interior decorator to discuss remodelling the bars. They were overdue for a little redesigning anyway, and it was high time I did some serious thinking about how I ran my business. Just as with people, with bars there's a time to leave them alone and a time for change. Being stuck in the same environment, you grow dull and lethargic. Your energy level takes a nosedive. Even castles in the air can do with a fresh coat of paint. I started with the other bar, saving the Robin's Nest for later. I began by removing all its hyper-chic aspects which, when you came down to it, were a pain in the backside, the whole point being to come up with an efficient, functional workplace. The audio system and air conditioning were due for an overhaul too, as was the menu, which I revamped drastically. I interviewed my employees and came up with a long list of suggested improvements. In great detail I laid out to the designer my vision of what the bar should be, got him to draw up a plan, then sent him back to the drawing board to incorporate features that had popped into my head in the meantime. We repeated this process a number of times. I selected all the materials, had the contractors draw up estimates, readjusted my budget. I spent three weeks scouring shops throughout Tokyo in search of the world's greatest soap dispenser. All of this kept me extremely busy. But that, after all, was precisely what I wanted.

May came and went, then it was June. Still no Shimamoto. I was sure she had gone for ever. *Probably I won't be able to come here for a while,* she'd written. It was this *probably* and *for a while* and the ambiguity inherent in them that made me suffer. Some day she might show up again. But I couldn't just sit around, resting my hopes and dreams on vague promises. Keep on like this, I thought, and I'll end up a blithering idiot, so I concentrated on keeping myself busy. I started going to the pool every morning and I'd swim two thousand metres without stopping, then go upstairs to the gym to do some weight lifting. A week of that and my muscles started to rebel. Waiting at a red light one day, I felt my left foot go numb and I couldn't let in the clutch. Finally, though, my muscles got used to the workout. Hard physical effort left no room to think and keeping my body always in motion helped me to focus on the trivia of daily life. Daydreaming was forbidden. I tried my best to concentrate on whatever I was doing. Washing my face, I thought about that; listening to music, I was all music. It was the only way I could survive.

In the summer, Yukiko and I often took the kids to our cottage in Hakone. Away from Tokyo, in the countryside, Yukiko and the children were relaxed and happy. They picked flowers, watched birds with binoculars, played tag, splashed about in the river. Or else they just lay around in the garden. But they didn't know the truth. That on a certain snowy winter day, if my plane had been grounded, I would have thrown them all away to be with Shimamoto. My job, my family, my money – everything, without flinching. And here I was, my head still full of Shimamoto. The sensation of holding her, of kissing her cheek, wouldn't leave me. I couldn't drive the image of Shimamoto from my mind and replace it with my wife. Just as I could never tell what Shimamoto was thinking, no one had a clue to what was in my mind.

I decided to spend the rest of our summer holiday finishing the remodelling. While Yukiko and the children were in Hakone, I stayed in Tokyo alone to supervise the work and give last-minute instructions. I'd swim in the pool, work out at the gym. On weekends I'd go to Hakone, swim in the Fujiya Hotel pool with my daughters and we'd all have dinner together. And at night I'd make love to my wife.

I was fast approaching middle age, yet had no extra fat to speak of, no thinning hair. Not a single white hair, either. Exercise helped to keep the inevitable physical decline at bay. Lead a well-regulated life, never overdo anything and watch your diet: that was my motto. I never got sick, and most people would have guessed I was barely thirty.

My wife loved to touch my body. She'd touch the muscles on my chest and stomach, and fondle my penis and balls. Yukiko, too, was going to the gym to work out regularly. But it didn't seem to slim her down.

"I must be getting old," she sighed. "My weight goes down, but this roll of flab is still here."

"I like your body just the way it is," I told her. "You're fine the way you are – no need to work out or go on diets. It's not as if you're fat or anything." Which wasn't a lie. I really did like the softness of her body with its bit of extra flesh. I loved to rub her naked back.

"You just don't understand," she said, shaking her head. "You say it's all right for me to look the way I am now, but it takes every ounce of energy I have just to stay in the same place."

An outsider would probably have said we had an ideal

135

life. Certainly I was convinced of it at times. I was enthusiastic about my work and was making a good deal of money. I owned a four-bedroomed apartment condo in Aoyama, a small cottage in the mountains of Hakone, a BMW, a Jeep Cherokee. And I had a happy family. I loved my wife and my two daughters. What more could anyone ask for? If, say, Yukiko and the children had begged me to tell them what they should do to be even better to me, to be loved even more, there was nothing I could have said. I could not imagine a happier life.

But since Shimamoto had stopped coming to see me, I was stuck on the airless surface of the moon. If she had gone for ever, no one remained to whom I could reveal my true feelings. On sleepless nights I'd lie in bed and replay over and over in my mind that scene at the snowy Komatsu Airport. Recall it enough times and the memories would start to fade. Or so I thought. The more I remembered, the stronger the memories became. The word "Delayed" flashing on the flight information board; outside the window, the snow coming down hard. You couldn't see more than fifty yards. On the bench, Shimamoto sat still, hugging herself tight. Her navy duffel coat and scarf. Her body with its mixed scent of tears and sadness. I could smell that scent. Beside me, in bed, my wife breathed quietly, asleep. She knows nothing. I closed my eyes and shook my head. *She knows nothing*.

The abandoned bowling alley car park, melting snow in my mouth and feeding it to her. Shimamoto in the plane, in my arms. Her closed eyes, the sigh from her slightly parted lips. Her body, soft and limp. She wanted me then. Her heart was open to me. Yet I held myself back, back on the surface of the moon, stuck in this lifeless world. And in the end she left me and my life was lost all over again.

Sometimes I'd wake up at two or three in the morning and

not be able to fall asleep again. I'd get out of bed, go to the kitchen and pour myself a whisky. Glass in hand, I'd look down at the darkened cemetery across the way and the headlights of the cars on the road. The moments of time linking night and dawn were long and dark. If I could cry, it might make things easier. But what would I cry over? Who would I cry for? I was too self-centred to cry for other people, too old to cry for myself.

Autumn finally arrived. And when it did, I came to a decision. Something had to give: I couldn't keep on living like this.

13

One morning after dropping off my daughters at nursery school, I went to the pool and swam my usual two thousand metres. I imagined I was a fish. Just a fish, with no need to think, not even about swimming. Then I showered, changed into a T-shirt and shorts and started pumping iron.

Afterwards I headed for the one-room flat I used as an office and started checking the accounts, working out my employees' pay, thinking about the plan for remodelling the Robin's Nest the following February. At one, as usual, I went home and had lunch with my wife.

"Darling, I had a call from my father this morning," Yukiko said. "Busy as always. He said there's this stock that'll go through the roof, and we should buy as much as we could manage. Not your run-of-the-mill stock tip, he said, but something extra special."

"If it's going to earn that much, he shouldn't tell us about it but keep it to himself. Wonder why he didn't."

"He said this was his personal way of saying thanks to you. He said you'd understand what he meant. Do you? He's letting us have his share, you see. He said to invest all the money we have and not to worry, because this stock was hot. If somehow it didn't turn a profit, he'd make sure we didn't lose a penny."

I rested my fork on my plate of pasta. "Anything else?"

"Well, he said we had to move quickly, so I called the bank and had them close our savings accounts and send the money to Mr Nakayama at the investment firm. So he could buy the stock. I was only able to scrape together about eight million yen. Maybe I should have bought more?"

I drank some water. And tried to find the right words. "Before you did all that, why didn't you ask me?"

"Ask you?" she said, surprised. "But you always buy the stock my father tells you to. You've asked me to do it any number of times, haven't you? You always tell me to just go ahead and do what I think is right. So that's what I did. My father said there wasn't a minute to lose. You were at the swimming pool and I couldn't get in touch with you. So what's the problem?"

"It's all right," I said. "But I want you to sell all the stock."

"*Sell it?*" She screwed up her eyes as if blinded by a glaring light.

"Sell all the stock you bought and put the money back in our savings accounts."

"But if I do that, we'll have to pay a lot in transaction fees."

"I don't care," I said. "Just pay it. I don't care if we end up losing. Just sell everything you bought today."

Yukiko sighed. "What happened between you and Father? What's going on?"

I didn't answer.

"What happened?"

139

"Listen, Yukiko," I began, "I'm getting sick of all this. I don't want to earn money in the stock market. I want to earn money by working with my own hands. I've done a good job up till now. You haven't wanted for money, have you?"

"I know you've done a good job, and I haven't complained once. I'm grateful to you and you know I respect you. But still my father's doing this to help us out. Don't you understand that?"

"I do understand. Yukiko, do you know what insider trading is? Do you know what it means when somebody tells you there's a one hundred per cent chance you'll make a profit?"

"No."

"It's called stock manipulation," I said. "Somebody inside a company manipulates the stock to make an artificial profit, then he and his mates split the proceeds. And that money makes its way into politicians' pockets or ends up as corporate bribes. This isn't like the kind of stock your father urged me to buy before. That stock *probably* was going to make a profit. That was just welcome information, nothing more. And most of the time the stock did go up, but not every time. This time is different. This stinks. And I don't want to have anything to do with it."

Fork in hand, Yukiko was lost in thought.

"How can you be sure this is a case of stock manipulation?"

"If you really want to know that, ask your father," I said. "But I can tell you this: stock that's guaranteed not to go down can only result from illegal deals. My father worked in a stockbroker's for forty years. Worked hard from morning to night. But all he left behind was a crummy little house. Maybe he just wasn't good at it. Every night, my mother was hunched over the household account books, worried over a hundred or two hundred yen that didn't balance. That's the

140

kind of family I was brought up in. You said you can only come up with eight million yen. Yukiko, we're talking about real money here, not Monopoly money. Most people ride to work every day, crowded together in packed trains, put in overtime, knock themselves out, and still couldn't come near to making that much in a year. I lived that kind of life for eight years, so I know. And there was no way I could make eight million yen. But you probably can't picture that kind of life."

Yukiko was silent. She bit her lip and stared hard at her plate. Realizing that I'd begun to raise my voice, I lowered it.

"You can blithely say that in a fortnight the money we invest will double. Eight million yen will turn into sixteen million. But something's very wrong with that kind of thinking. I've found myself sucked into that mindset, and it makes me feel empty."

Yukiko looked at me across the table. As I resumed eating, I could feel something inside me shaking. Was it irritation or anger? I couldn't tell. Whatever it was, I was helpless before it.

"I'm sorry. I should have minded my own business," Yukiko said quietly, after a long silence.

"It's OK. I'm not blaming you. I'm not blaming anybody."

"I'll phone them straight away and tell them to sell every single share. Just stop being angry with me."

"I'm not angry."

Silent, I continued to eat.

"Isn't there something you want to tell me?" Yukiko asked, looking straight at me. "If something is bothering you, tell me. Even if it's something that's hard to talk about. If there's anything I can do, just name it. I'm only an ordinary person, and I know I'm completely naive about everything – including running a business. But I can't stand to see you unhappy. I don't want to see that pained look on your face. What is it you hate about our life? Tell me."

I shook my head. "I have no complaints. I like my job and I love you. All I'm saying is that sometimes I can't keep up with your father's way of doing things. Don't get me wrong, I like him. I know he's trying to help us out and I appreciate it. So I'm not angry. I just can't understand who I am any more. I can't tell right from wrong. So I'm confused. But not angry."

"You certainly look angry."

I sighed.

"And you sigh all the time," she said. "Anyhow, something's definitely bothering you. Your mind's a million miles away."

"I don't know."

Yukiko kept her eyes on me. "There's something on your mind," she said. "But I have no idea what it is. I wish there was something I could do to help."

I was struck by a violent desire to confess everything. What a relief that would be! No more hiding, no more need to playact or to lie. *Yukiko, look, there's another woman I love, someone I just can't forget. I've held back, trying to keep our world from crumbling, but I can't hold back any more. The next time she shows up, I don't care what happens: I'm going to make love to her. I've thought of her while I've masturbated. I've thought of her while I've made love to you, Yukiko . . .* But I didn't say anything. Confession would serve no purpose. It would only make us miserable.

After lunch, I returned to my office to continue working. But my mind was a million miles away. I felt miserable, preaching at Yukiko like that. *What* I said was all right. But the person who said it was all wrong. I'd lied to Yukiko, sneaking around behind her back. I was the last person who should take the moral high ground. Yukiko was trying very hard to think

142

about me. That was quite clear and consistent with the kind of person she was. But what about my life? Was there any consistency, any conviction to speak of? I felt deflated, utterly lacking the will to move.

I put my feet up on my desk and, pencil in hand, gazed listlessly out of the window. From my office you could see a park. The weather was nice, and there were a number of parents with their children. The children played in the sand pit or slid down the slides, while their mothers kept an eye on them and chatted with other mothers. Seeing them reminded me of my own daughters. I wanted to see them, to walk down the street holding the two of them in my arms once again. I wanted to feel the warmth of their bodies. But thoughts of them led inexorably to memories of Shimamoto. Vivid memories of her slightly parted lips. Thoughts of my daughters were crowded out by the image of Shimamoto. I could think of nothing else.

I left my office and walked down the main street in Aoyama. I went into the café where Shimamoto and I used to meet, and had a coffee. I read a book and, when I tired of reading, thought again of her. I recalled fragments of our conversations, how she'd take a Salem out of her bag and light it, how she'd casually brush back a lock of hair, how she tilted her head slightly as she smiled. Soon I grew tired of sitting there alone and set out towards Shibuya. I used to like walking the city streets, gazing at the buildings and shops, watching all the people. I liked the feeling of moving through the city on my own two feet. Now, though, the city was depressing and empty. Buildings were falling apart, all the trees had lost their colour, and every passer-by was devoid of feelings, and of dreams.

Looking for an unpopular film, I entered the cinema and watched the screen intently. When the show was over, I

143

walked out into the evening city streets, went into a restaurant I happened to pass and had a simple meal. Shibuya was packed with office workers on their way home. Like a speeded-up film, trains pulled into the station and swallowed up one crowd after another. It was right around here, I suddenly recalled, that I'd caught sight of Shimamoto, some ten years before, in her red overcoat and sunglasses. It might have been a million years ago.

Everything came back to me. The end-of-year crowds, the way she walked, each corner we turned, the cloudy sky, the department store bag she carried, the coffee cup she didn't touch, the Christmas carols. Once again a pang of regret swept over me for not having called out to her. I had had nothing to tie me down then, nothing to lose. I could have held her close, and the two of us could have walked off together. No matter what situation she was stuck in, we could have found a way out. But I'd lost that chance for ever. A mysterious middle-aged man grabbed me by the elbow, and Shimamoto slipped into a taxi and disappeared.

I took a crowded evening train back. The weather had taken a turn for the worse while I was watching the film, and the sky was covered with heavy, wet-looking clouds. It looked like it was going to rain at any minute. I had no umbrella with me and was dressed in the sailing jacket, blue jeans and trainers I'd set out in that morning when I went to the pool. I should have gone home to change into my usual suit. But I didn't feel like it. It didn't matter, I'd decided. I could leave off the tie for once – no harm would be done.

By seven it was raining. A gentle rain, the kind of autumn drizzle that looked like it would last. As I usually did, I stopped by the remodelled bar first to check out how business was. The place had ended up pretty much as I had imagined it. It was a much more relaxed, efficient place to work. The lighting was more subdued and the music enhanced this mood. I had designed a small separate kitchen, hired a professional chef and made up a new menu of simple yet elegant dishes. The kind of dishes that had no extra ingredients or flourishes but which an amateur could never master. They were intended, after all, as snacks to accompany drinks, so they had to be easy to eat. Every month we changed the menu completely. It had been no easy task to find the kind of chef I had in mind. I finally located one, though it cost me much more than I'd bargained for. But he earned his pay and I was satisfied. My customers seemed pleased too.

Around nine, I borrowed an umbrella from the bar and headed over to the Robin's Nest. And at nine-thirty Shimamoto showed up. Strangely enough, she always appeared on quiet, rainy evenings.

14

She wore a white dress and an oversized navy-blue jacket. A small fish-shaped silver brooch graced its collar. The dress was simple in design, with no decorations of any kind, yet on her you'd swear it was the world's most expensive dress. She was more tanned than the last time I'd seen her.

"I thought you'd never come here again," I said.

"Every time I see you, you say the same thing," she said, laughing. As always, she sat down next to me at the bar and rested both hands on the counter. "But I did write you a note saying I wouldn't be back for a while, didn't I?"

"*For a while* is a phrase whose length can't be measured. At least by the person who's waiting," I said.

"But there must be times when that word's necessary. Situations when that's the only possible word you can use," she said.

"And *probably* is a word whose weight is incalculable."

"You're right," she said, her face lit up by her usual smile, a gentle breeze blowing from somewhere far away. "I apologize. I'm not trying to excuse myself, but there was nothing I could do about it. Those were the only words I could have used."

"No need to apologize. As I told you once, this is a bar and you're a customer. You come here when you want to. I'm used to it. I'm just mouthing off to myself. Pay no attention."

She called the bartender over and ordered a cocktail. She looked closely at me, as if inspecting me. "You're dressed pretty casually for a change."

"I went swimming this morning and haven't changed. I haven't had time," I said. "But I quite like it. I feel this is the real me again."

"You look younger. No one would guess you're thirty-seven."

"You don't look thirty-seven, either."

"But I don't look twelve."

"True enough," I said.

Her cocktail arrived and she took a sip. And gently closed her eyes as if listening to some far-off sound. With her eyes closed, I could once more make out the small line just above her eyelids.

"Hajime," she said, "I've been thinking about your bar's cocktails. I really wanted to have one. No matter where you go, you can never find drinks like the ones here."

"Did you go somewhere far away?"

"Why do you say that?" she asked.

"Something about you," I replied. "A certain air. Like you've been gone for some time far away."

She looked up at me. And nodded. "Hajime, for a long time I've . . . ", she began, but fell suddenly silent, as if reminded of something. I could tell she was searching inside herself for the right words. Which she couldn't find. She bit her lip and

147

smiled once more. "Anyhow, I'm sorry. I should have got in touch with you. But I wanted to leave certain things as they are. Preserved, so to speak. Either I come here or I don't. When I do come here, I do. When I don't . . . I'm somewhere else."

"There's no middle ground?"

"No middle ground," she said. "Why? Because no middle-ground things exist there."

"In a place where there are no middle-ground objects, no middle ground exists," I said.

"Exactly."

"In a place where no dogs exist, there are no doghouses, in other words."

"Yes; no dogs, no doghouses," Shimamoto said. And she looked at me in a funny way. "You have a strange sense of humour, do you know that?"

As it often did, the piano trio began playing "Star-Crossed Lovers". For a while the two of us sat there, listening silently.

"Mind if I ask you one question?"

"Not at all," I said.

"What is it with you and this song?" she asked. "Every time you're here, it seems, they play that number. A house rule of some sort?"

"No. They just know I like it."

"It is a beautiful song."

I nodded. "It took me a long time to work out how complex it is, how there's so much more to it than just a pretty melody. It takes a special kind of musician to play it right," I said. "Duke Ellington and Billy Strayhorn wrote it a long time ago. Fifty-seven, I believe."

"When they say 'star-crossed', what do they mean?"

"You know – lovers born under an unlucky star. Unlucky lovers. Here it's referring to Romeo and Juliet. Ellington

148

and Strayhorn wrote it for a performance at the Ontario Shakespeare Festival. In the original recording, Johnny Hodges' alto sax was Juliet, and Paul Gonsalves played the Romeo part on tenor sax."

"Lovers born under an unlucky star," she said. "Sounds like it was written for the two of us."

"You mean we're lovers?"

"You think we're not?"

I looked at her. She wasn't smiling any more. I could make out a faint glimmer deep within her eyes.

"Shimamoto-san, I don't know anything about you," I said. "Every time I look in your eyes, I feel that. The most I can say about you is how you were at age twelve. The Shimamoto-san who lived in the neighbourhood and was in my class. But that was twenty-five years ago. The Twist was in, and people still rode on trams. No cassette tapes, no tampons, no bullet train, no diet food. I'm talking about a long time ago. Other than what I know about you then, I'm in the dark."

"Is that what you see in my eyes? That you know nothing about me?"

"Nothing's written in your eyes," I replied. "It's written in *my* eyes. I just see the reflection in yours."

"Hajime," she said, "I know I should be telling you more. I do. There's nothing I can do about it. So please don't say anything further."

"As I said, I'm just mouthing off to myself. Don't give it a second thought."

She raised a hand to her collar and fingered the fish brooch. And quietly listened to the piano trio. When their performance ended, she clapped and took a sip of her cocktail. Finally she let out a long sigh and turned to me. "Six months is a long time," she said. "But most likely, probably, I'll be able to come here for a while."

"The old magic words," I said.

"Magic words?"

"*Probably* and *for a while*."

She smiled and looked at me. She took a cigarette out of her small bag and lit it with a lighter.

"Sometimes when I look at you, I feel I'm gazing at a distant star," I said. "It's dazzling, but the light is from tens of thousands of years ago. Maybe the star doesn't even exist any more. Yet sometimes that light seems more real to me than anything."

Shimamoto said nothing.

"You're here," I continued. "At least you look as if you're here. But maybe you aren't. Maybe it's just your shadow. The real you may be somewhere else. Or maybe you already disappeared, a long, long time ago. I reach out my hand to see, but you've hidden yourself behind a cloud of *probablys*. Do you think we can go on like this for ever?"

"Possibly. For the time being," she answered.

"I see I'm not the only one with a strange sense of humour," I said. And smiled.

She smiled too. The rain has stopped, without a sound there's a break in the clouds, and the very first rays of sunlight shine through – that kind of smile. Small, warm lines at the corners of her eyes, holding out the promise of something wonderful.

"Hajime," she said, "I brought you a present."

She passed me a beautifully wrapped package with a red bow.

"Looks like a record," I said, gauging its size and shape.

"It's a Nat King Cole record. The one we used to listen to together. Remember? I'm giving it to you."

"Thanks. But don't you want it? As a keepsake from your father?"

"I have more. This one's for you."

I gazed at the record, wrapped and beribboned. Before long, all the sounds around me – the clamour of the people at the bar, the piano trio's music – all faded into the distance, as if the tide had gone out. Only she and I remained. Everything else was an illusion, papier-mâché props on a stage. What existed, what was *real*, was the two of us.

"Shimamoto-san," I said, "why don't we go somewhere and listen to this together?"

"That would be wonderful," she said.

"I have a small cottage in Hakone. It's empty now, and there's a stereo there. At this time of night we could drive there in an hour and a half."

She looked at her watch. And then at me. "You want to go there now?"

"Yes," I said.

She narrowed her eyes. "But it's already past ten. If we went to Hakone now, it would be very late when we came back. Don't you mind?"

"No. Do you?"

Once more she looked at her watch. And closed her eyes for a good ten seconds. When she reopened them, her face was filled with an entirely new expression, as if she'd gone far away, left something there, and returned. "All right," she said. "Let's go."

I phoned the acting manager and asked him to take care of things in my absence – lock up the till, organize the receipts and put the profits in the bank's overnight deposit box. I walked over to my apartment and drove the BMW out of the underground garage. And called my wife from a nearby telephone booth, telling her I was off to Hakone.

"At this hour?" she said, surprised. "Why do you have to

go all the way to Hakone at this hour?"

"There's something I need to think over," I said.

"So you won't be back tonight?"

"Probably not."

"Darling, I've been thinking over what happened, and I'm really sorry. You were right. I got rid of all the stock. So why don't you come home?"

"Yukiko, I'm not angry at you. Not at all. Forget about that. I just want some time to think. Give me one night, OK?"

She said nothing for a while. Then: "All right." She sounded exhausted. "Go to Hakone. But be careful driving. It's raining."

"I will."

"There's so much I don't understand," my wife said. "Tell me one thing: am I in your way?"

"Not at all," I replied. "It has nothing to do with you. If anything, the problem's with me. So don't worry about it, OK? I just want some time to think."

I hung up and drove to the bar. I could tell from Yukiko's voice that she'd been mulling over our lunchtime conversation. She was tired, confused. It saddened me. The rain was still falling hard. I let Shimamoto into the car.

"Don't you need to phone somewhere before we go?" I asked.

Silently she shook her head. And, as she did on the way back from Haneda Airport, she pressed her face against the glass and stared outside.

There was little traffic on the way to Hakone. I turned off the Tomei Highway at Atsugi and headed straight to Odawara on the motorway. I kept our speed between eighty and ninety miles per hour. The rain came down in sheets from time to time, but I knew every curve and hill along the way. Once we were on the motorway, Shimamoto and I said hardly a word.

I played a Mozart quartet quietly and kept my eyes on the road. Shimamoto was lost in thought as she looked out the window. Occasionally she'd glance at me. Whenever she did, my throat went dry. I swallowed a couple of times, forcing myself to relax.

"Hajime," she said. We were near Kouzu. "You don't listen to jazz much outside the bar?"

"No, I don't. Mostly classical music."

"Why?"

"I suppose because jazz is part of my job. Outside the club, I like to listen to something different. Sometimes rock too, but hardly ever jazz."

"What type of music does your wife listen to?"

"Usually whatever I'm listening to. She hardly ever plays any records on her own. I'm not even sure if she knows how to use the turntable."

Shimamoto reached over to the cassette case and pulled out a couple of tapes. One of them contained the children's songs my daughters and I sang together in the car. "The Doggy Policeman" and "Tulip". From her expression as she gazed at the cassette and its picture of Snoopy on the cover, you'd think she'd discovered something from outer space.

Again she turned to gaze at me. "Hajime," she said after a while. "When I look at you driving, sometimes I want to grab the steering wheel and give it a yank. It would kill us, wouldn't it?"

"We'd die, for sure. We're going at eighty miles an hour."

"You'd rather not die with me?"

"I can think of more pleasant ways to go." I laughed. "And besides, we haven't listened to the record yet. That's the reason we're here, isn't it?"

"Don't worry," she said. "I won't do anything like that. The thought just crosses my mind from time to time."

It was only the beginning of October, but nights in Hakone were chilly. We arrived at the cottage and I turned on the lights and lit the gas stove in the living room. And took down a bottle of brandy and two glasses from the shelf. We sat next to each other on the sofa, as we used to do so many years before, and I put the Nat King Cole record on the turntable. The red glow from the stove was reflected in our brandy glasses. Shimamoto sat with her legs folded underneath her. She rested one arm on the back of the sofa, the other in her lap. The same as in the old days. Then she had probably wanted to hide her leg and the habit remained even now. Nat King Cole was singing "South of the Border". How many years was it since I had heard that tune?

"When I was a kid and listened to this record, I used to wonder what it was that lay south of the border," I said.

"Me too," she said. "When I grew up and could read the English lyrics, I was disappointed. It was just a song about Mexico. I'd always thought something great was south of the border."

"What, for example?"

Shimamoto brushed her hair back and lightly gathered it behind her head. "I'm not sure. Something beautiful, big and soft."

"Something beautiful, big and soft," I repeated. "Was it edible?"

She laughed. Her white teeth showed faintly. "I doubt it."

"Something you can touch?"

"Probably."

"Again with the *probably*s."

"A world full of *probably*s," she said.

I stretched out my hand and laid it on top of her fingers on the back of the sofa. I hadn't touched her body for so very

154

long, not since the flight back from Ishikawa. As my fingers grazed hers, she looked up at me briefly, then down again.

"South of the border, west of the sun," she said.

"West of the sun?"

"Have you heard of the illness *hysteria siberiana*?"

"No."

"I read this somewhere a long time ago. Maybe in junior high. I can't for the life of me recall what book I read it in. Anyway, it affects farmers living in Siberia. Try to imagine this. You're a farmer, living all alone on the Siberian tundra. Day after day you plough your fields. As far as the eye can see, nothing. To the north, the horizon, to the east, the horizon, to the south, to the west, more of the same. Every morning, when the sun rises in the east, you go out to work in your fields. When it's directly overhead, you take a break for lunch. When it sinks in the west, you go home to sleep."

"Not exactly the lifestyle of an Aoyama bar owner."

"Hardly." She smiled and inclined her head ever so slightly. "Anyway, that cycle continues, year after year."

"But in Siberia they don't work in the fields in winter."

"They rest in the winter," she said. "In the winter they stay at home and do indoor work. When spring comes, they go out into the fields again. You're that farmer. Imagine it."

"OK," I said.

"And then one day something inside you dies."

"What do you mean?"

She shook her head. "I don't know. Something. Day after day you watch the sun rise in the east, pass across the sky, then sink in the west, and something breaks inside you and dies. You throw your plough aside and, your head completely empty of thought, you begin walking toward the west. Heading toward a land that lies west of the sun. Like someone possessed, you walk on, day after day, not

155

eating or drinking, until you collapse on the ground and die. That's *hysteria siberiana*."

I tried to conjure up the picture of a Siberian farmer lying dead on the ground.

"But what is there, west of the sun?" I asked.

She shook her head again. "I don't know. Maybe nothing. Or maybe *something*. At any rate, it's different from south of the border."

When Nat King Cole began singing "Pretend", Shimamoto, as she had done so very long before, sang along in a small voice.

> *Pretend you're happy when you're blue*
> *It isn't very hard to do*

"Shimamoto-san," I said, "after you left, I thought about you for a long time. Every day for six months, from morning to night. I tried to stop, but I couldn't. And I came to this conclusion. I can't make it without you. I don't ever want to lose you again. I don't want to hear the words *for a while* any more. Or *probably*. You'll say we can't see each other for a while and then you'll disappear. And no one can say when you'll be back. You might never be back and I might spend the rest of my life never seeing you again. And I couldn't stand that. Life would be meaningless."

Shimamoto looked at me without speaking, still smiling. A quiet smile that nothing could ever touch, revealing nothing to me of what lay beyond. Confronted with that smile, I felt as if my own emotions were about to be lost to me. For an instant I lost my bearings, my sense of who and where I was. After a while, though, words returned.

"I love you," I told her. "Nothing can change it. Special feelings like that should never, ever be taken away. I've lost you many times. But I should never have let you go. These

156

last few months have taught me that. I love you and I don't want you ever to leave me."

When I finished, she closed her eyes. The fire from the stove burned and Nat King Cole kept on singing his old songs. I should say something more, I thought, but I could think of nothing.

"Hajime," she began, "this is very important, so listen carefully. As I told you before, there is no middle ground with me. You take either all of me or nothing. That's the way it works. If you don't mind continuing the way we are now, I don't see why we can't do that. I don't know how long we'd be able to, but I'll do everything in my power to see that it happens. When I'm able to come and see you, I will. But when I can't, I can't. I can't just come whenever I feel like it. You may not be satisfied with that arrangement, but if you don't want me to go away again, you have to take all of me. Everything. All the baggage I carry, everything that clings to me. And I will take all of you. Do you understand that? *Do you understand what that means?*"

"Yes," I said.

"And you still want to be with me?"

"I've already decided, Shimamoto-san," I said. "I thought about it when you had gone, and I made my decision."

"But, Hajime, you have a wife and two children. And you love them. You want to do what's right for them."

"Of course I love them. Very much. And I want to take care of them. But something's missing. I have a family, a job, and no complaints about either. You could say I'm happy. Yet I've known ever since I met you again that something is missing. The important question is *what* is missing. Something's lacking. In me and my life. And that part of me is always hungry, always thirsting. Neither my wife nor my children can fill that gap. In the whole world, there's only one person who can do that. You. Only now, when that thirst is satisfied, do I realize how empty I was. And how I've been hungering, thirsting, for so many years. I can't go back to that kind of world."

Shimamoto wrapped both her arms around me and rested her head on my shoulder. I could feel the softness of her body. It pushed against me warmly, insistently.

"I love you too, Hajime. You're the only person I've ever loved. I don't think you realize how very much I love you. I've loved you ever since I was twelve. Whenever anyone else held me, I thought of you. And that's the reason why I didn't want to see you again. If I saw you once, I knew I couldn't stand it any more. But I couldn't keep myself away. At first I thought I'd just make sure it was really you, then go home. But once I saw you I had to talk to you." She kept her head on my shoulder. "Ever since I was twelve, I have wanted you to hold me. You never knew that, did you?"

"No, I didn't," I admitted.

"Since I was twelve, I have wanted to hold you, naked. You had no idea, I suppose."

I held her close and kissed her. She closed her eyes, not moving. Our tongues wound round each other and I could feel her heartbeat just below her breasts. A passionate, warm heartbeat. I closed my eyes and thought of the red blood coursing through her veins. I stroked her soft hair and drank in its fragrance. Her hands wandered over my back. The record finished and the arm moved back to its base. Once again we were wrapped only in the sound of the rain. After a while, she opened her eyes. "Hajime," she whispered, "are you sure this is all right? Are you sure you want to throw away everything for my sake?"

I nodded. "Yes. I've already made up my mind."

"But if you'd never met me, you could have had a peaceful

life. With no doubts or dissatisfactions. Don't you think so?"

"Maybe. But I *did* meet you. And we can't undo that," I said. "Just as you told me once, there are certain things you can't undo. You can only go forward. Shimamoto-san, I don't care where we end up; I just know I want to go there with you. And begin again."

"Hajime," she said, "would you take off your clothes and let me see your body?"

"You want just me to take off my clothes?"

"Yes. First you take all your clothes off. I want to look at your body. You don't want to?"

"I don't mind. If you want me to," I said. I undressed in front of the stove. I took off my sailing jacket, polo shirt, blue jeans, socks, T-shirt, pants. Shimamoto made me get down on both knees on the floor. My penis was already hard, which embarrassed me a little. She moved back slightly to take in the scene. She still wore her jacket.

"It seems strange to be the only naked one." I laughed.

"It's lovely, Hajime," she said. She came close to me, gently cradled my penis in her hand and kissed me on the lips. She put her hands on my chest and for the longest time licked my nipples and stroked my pubic hair. She put her ear to my navel and took my balls in her mouth. She kissed me all over. Even the soles of my feet. It was as if she were treasuring time itself. Stroking time, caressing it, licking it.

"Aren't you going to undress?" I asked.

"Later on," she replied. "I want to enjoy looking at your body first, touching and licking it as much as I want to. If I got undressed now, you'd want to touch me, wouldn't you? Even if I told you not to, you wouldn't be able to restrain yourself."

"You're right about that."

"I don't want to do it that way. It took us long enough to

159

get here and I want to take it nice and slowly. I want to look at you, touch you with these hands, lick you with my tongue. I want to try everything – *slowly*. If I don't, I can't go on to the next stage. Hajime, if what I do seems a little odd, don't worry about it, all right? I have to. Don't say anything, just let me do it."

"I don't mind. Do whatever you like. But I do feel a bit weird being stared at like this."

"But you are mine, right?"

"Yes."

"So there's nothing to be embarrassed about, is there?"

"I suppose you're right," I said. "I'll have to get used to it."

"Just be patient a little bit longer. This has been my dream for such a very long time."

"Looking at my body has been your dream? Touching me all over, with all your clothes still on?"

"Yes," she answered. "I've been imagining your body for ages. What your penis looked like, how hard it would get, how big."

"Why did you think of that?"

"Why?" she asked incredulously. "I told you I love you. What's wrong with thinking about the body of the man you love? Haven't you thought about my body?"

"I have," I said.

"I bet you've thought about my body while you're masturbating."

"Yes. In junior high and high school," I said, then corrected myself. "Well, actually, not too long ago."

"It's the same with me. I've thought about your body. Women do too, you know," she said.

I pulled her close to me again and kissed her slowly. Her tongue slid languidly inside my mouth. "I love you, Shimamoto-san," I said.

"I love you, Hajime," she said. "There's no one else I love but you. May I see your body a little more?"

"Go ahead," I replied.

She gently wrapped her palm around my penis and balls. "It's wonderful," she said. "I'd like to eat it all up."

"Then what would I do?"

"But I do want to eat it up," she said. As if weighing them, she kept my balls in her palm for a long, long time. And licked and sucked my penis very slowly, very carefully. She looked at me. "The first time, can I do it the way I want to? You'll let me?"

"I don't mind. Do whatever you want," I said. "Except for eating me up, of course."

"I'm a little embarrassed, so don't say anything, all right?"

"I won't," I promised.

As I knelt on the floor, she put her left hand around my waist. She kept her dress on but with her other hand peeled off her stockings and knickers. Then she took my penis and balls in her right hand and licked them. Her other hand she slid under her dress. Sucking on my penis, she began to move her other hand around slowly.

I didn't say a thing. I guessed this was her way. I watched the movements of her lips and tongue and the slow motion of her hand beneath her skirt. Suddenly I remembered the Shimamoto I'd seen in the car park of the bowling alley – stiff and white as a sheet. I recalled clearly what I'd seen deep within her eyes. A dark space, frozen hard like a subterranean glacier. A silence so profound it sucked up every sound, never allowing it to resurface. Absolute, total silence.

It was the first time I'd been face to face with death. So I'd had no distinct image of what death really was. But there it was then, right before my eyes, spread out just inches from my face. So this is the face of death, I'd thought. And death spoke to me, saying that my time, too, would one day come. Eventually everyone would fall into those endlessly lonely depths, the source of all darkness, a silence bereft of resonance. I felt choking, stifling fear as I stared into a bottomless dark pit.

Facing those black, frozen depths, I had called out her name. *Shimamoto-san*, I had called out again and again. But my voice was lost in that infinite nothingness. Cry out as I might, nothing within the depths of her eyes changed. Her breathing remained strange, like the sound of wind whipping through cracks. Her regular breaths told me she was still on this side of the world. But her eyes told me she was already given up to death.

As I had looked deep into her eyes and called out her name, my own body was dragged down into those depths. As if a vacuum had sucked out all the air around me, that other world was steadily pulling me closer. Even now I could feel its power. It wanted *me*.

I closed my eyes tight. And drove those memories from my mind.

I reached out and stroked her hair. I touched her ears, rested my hand on her forehead. Her body was warm and soft. She sucked on my penis as if trying to suck out life itself. Her hand, communicating in some secret sign language, continued to move between her legs, under her skirt. A short time later, I came in her mouth; her hand under her skirt ceased moving and she closed her eyes. She swallowed down the very last drop of my semen.

"I'm sorry," Shimamoto said.

"There's nothing to apologize for," I said.

"The first time, I wanted to do it this way," she said. "It's embarrassing, but I needed to. It's a rite of passage for the two of us, I suppose. Do you know what I mean?"

I pulled her to me and rubbed my cheek against hers. Her cheek felt warm. I lifted up her hair and kissed her ear. And looked into her eyes. I could see my face reflected in them. Deep within her eyes, in the always bottomless depths, there was a spring. And, ever so far off, a light. The light of life, I thought. Someday it will be extinguished, but for now the light is there. She smiled at me. The usual small creases formed at the corners of her eyes. I kissed the tiny lines.

"Now it's your turn to take off my clothes," she told me. "And do whatever you want."

"Maybe I'm not very imaginative, but I just like the regular way. All right?" I said.

"That's all right," she said. "I like it too."

I took off her dress and her bra, laid her on the bed and kissed her all over. I looked at every inch of her body, touching everywhere, kissing everywhere. Trying to find out everything and store it in my memory. It was a leisurely exploration. We had taken so very long to arrive at this point and, like her, the last thing I wanted to do was hurry. I held off as long as I could, until I couldn't stand it any more. Then I slowly slid inside her.

We fell asleep just before dawn. I don't know how many times we made love, sometimes gently, sometimes passionately. Once, in the midst of it, when I was inside her, she became possessed, crying violently and pounding on my back with her fists. All the while, I held her tightly to me. If I didn't hold her tight, I felt, she would fly off in pieces. I stroked her back over and over to calm her. I kissed her neck and brushed her hair with my fingers. She was no longer the cool, self-controlled Shimamoto I knew. The frozen hardness within her was, bit by bit, melting and floating to the surface. I could feel its breath, far-off signs of its presence.

I held her close and let her trembling seep inside me. Little by little, this is how she would become mine.

"I want to know everything there is to know about you," I said to her. "What kind of life you've had till now, where you live. Whether you're married or not. Everything. No more secrets, because I can't take any more."

"Tomorrow," she said. "Tomorrow I'll tell you everything. So don't ask till then. Stay the way you are today. If I did tell you now, you'd never be able to go back to the way you were."

"I'm not going back anyway. And who knows, tomorrow might never come. If it doesn't, I'll end up never knowing."

"I wish tomorrow would never come," she said. "Then you'd never know."

I was about to speak, but she hushed me up with a kiss.

"I wish a bald vulture would gobble up tomorrow," she said. "Would it make sense for a bald vulture to do that?"

"That makes sense. Bald vultures eat up art, and tomorrows as well."

"And ordinary vultures eat – "

" – the bodies of nameless people," I said. "Very different from bald vultures."

"Bald vultures eat up art and tomorrows, then?"

"Right."

"A nice combination."

"And for dessert they take a bite out of *Books in Print*."

Shimamoto laughed. "Anyhow, until tomorrow," she said.

And tomorrow came. When I woke up, I was alone. The rain had stopped and bright, transparent morning light shone in through the bedroom window. The clock showed it was after nine. Shimamoto wasn't in bed, though a small depression in the pillow beside me hinted at where she had been. She was nowhere to be seen. I got out of bed and went to the living room to look for her. I looked in the kitchen, the children's room and the bathroom. Nothing. Her clothes were gone, her shoes as well. I took a deep breath, trying to pull myself back to reality. But that reality was like nothing I'd ever seen before: a reality that didn't seem to fit.

I dressed and went outside. The BMW was parked where I had left it the night before. Maybe she'd woken early and gone out for a walk. I searched for her all around the house, then got in the car and drove as far as the nearest town. But no Shimamoto. I went back to the cottage, but she was not there. Thinking she might have left a note, I scoured the house. But there was nothing. Not a trace that she had ever been there.

Without her, the house was empty and stifling. The air was filled with a gritty layer of dust, which stuck in my throat with each breath. I remembered the record, the old Nat King Cole record she gave me. But search as I might, it was nowhere to be found. She must have taken it with her.

Once again Shimamoto had disappeared from my life. This time, though, leaving nothing to pin my hopes on. No more *probablys*. No more *for a whiles*.

15

I got back to Tokyo a little before four. Hoping against hope that Shimamoto would return, I had stayed at the cottage in Hakone until past noon. Waiting was torture, so I killed time by cleaning the kitchen and rearranging all the clothes in the house. The silence was oppressive; the occasional sounds of birds and cars struck me as unnatural, out of sync. Every sound was twisted and crushed beneath the weight of some unstoppable force. And in the midst of this, I waited for something to happen. *Something* must happen, I felt sure. It can't end like this.

But nothing happened. Once she made up her mind, Shimamoto wasn't the type of woman to change it. I had to get back to Tokyo. It seemed far-fetched, but if she did try to get in touch with me, she'd do it through the club. At any rate, staying in the cottage any longer made no sense.

Driving back, I had to force myself to concentrate. I missed curves, nearly went through red lights and swerved into the wrong lane. When I arrived at the club car park, I called home from a payphone. I told Yukiko I was back and that I was going straight to work.

"You had me worried. At least you could have called." Her voice sounded hard and dry.

"I'm fine. Not to worry," I said. I had no idea how my voice sounded to her. "I don't have much time, so I'm going to the office to check the accounts, and then directly on to the club."

At the office, I sat at my desk and somehow managed to pass the time until evening. I went over the previous night's events. Shimamoto must have got up while I was asleep and, without sleeping a wink herself, left before dawn. How she got back to the city I had no idea. The main road was a long way away, and at that hour of the morning it would have been almost impossible to get a bus or taxi in the hills around Hakone. And, besides, she had on high heels.

Why did Shimamoto have to leave me like that? The whole time I was driving back to Tokyo, the question had tormented me. I had told her I would be hers and she had said she'd be mine. And, dropping all defences, we made love. Still, she left me alone, without so much as a word of explanation. She'd even taken the record she had said was a present. There had to be some rhyme or reason to her actions, but logical thinking was beyond me. All trains of thought were sidetracked. Forcing myself to think, I ended up with a dully throbbing head. I realized how worn out I was. I sat down on the bed in my office, leaned against the wall and closed my eyes. Once they were closed, I couldn't pry them open. All I could do was remember. Like an endless tape loop, memories of the night before replayed themselves, over and over. Shimamoto's body. Her naked body as she lay by the stove with her eyes closed, and every detail – her neck, her breasts, her sides, her pubic hair, her genitals, her back, her waist, her legs. They were all too close, too clear. Clearer and closer than if they were real.

Alone in that tiny room, I was soon driven to distraction by these graphic illusions. I fled the building and wandered aimlessly. Finally I went over to the club and shaved in the cloakroom. I hadn't washed my face the whole day. And I was still wearing the same clothes as the day before. My employees said nothing, though I could feel them glancing at me strangely. If I went home now and stood before Yukiko, I knew I would confess. How I loved Shimamoto, had spent the night with her and was about to throw away everything – my home, my daughters, my work.

I know I should have told Yukiko everything. But I couldn't. Not then. I no longer had the power to distinguish right from wrong, or even to grasp what had happened to me. So I didn't go home. I went to the club and waited for Shimamoto, knowing full well my wait would be in vain. First I checked at the other bar to see if she was there, then I waited at the Robin's Nest until the place closed. I talked to a few of the regulars, but it was just so much background static. I made the appropriate listening noises, my head filled all the while with Shimamoto's body. How her vagina welcomed me ever so gently. And how she called out my name. Every time the phone rang my heart pounded.

After the bar closed and everyone had headed home, I stayed there at the counter, drinking. No matter how much I drank, I couldn't get drunk. In fact, the more I drank, the clearer my head became. It was two a.m. when I arrived home and Yukiko was up and waiting for me. Unable to sleep, I sat drinking whisky alone at the kitchen table. She came in with her glass to join me.

"Put on some music," she said. I picked up a nearby cassette, flipped it into the player and turned down the volume so as not to wake the children. We sat in silence for a while across the table from each other, drinking whisky.

"Presumably you have somebody else you like," Yukiko said, staring straight at me.

I nodded. Her words had a decided outline and gravity. How many times had she gone over them in her mind in preparation for this moment?

"And you really like that person. You're not just playing around."

"That's right," I said. "It's not just some fling. But it's not exactly what you're imagining."

"How do *you* know what I'm thinking?" she asked. "You actually believe you know what I'm thinking?"

I couldn't say a thing. Yukiko was silent too. The music played on softly. Vivaldi or Telemann. One of them. I couldn't recall the melody.

"I think it's likely you have no idea what I'm thinking," she said. She spoke slowly, enunciating each word distinctly, as if explaining something to the children. "I don't think you have any idea."

Seeing that I wasn't going to respond, she lifted her glass and drank. And very slowly, she shook her head. "I hope you know I'm not that stupid. I live with you, sleep with you. I've known for some time you like someone else."

I looked at her in silence.

"I'm not blaming you," she continued. "If you love someone else, there's not much anyone can do about it. You love who you love. I'm not enough for you. I know that. We've got on well together and you've taken good care of me. I've been very happy living with you. I think you still love me, but we can't escape the fact that I'm not enough for you. I knew this was going to happen. So I'm not blaming you for falling in love with another woman. I'm not angry, either. I should be, but I'm not. I just feel pain. A lot of pain. I thought I could imagine how much this would hurt, but I was wrong."

"I'm sorry," I said.

"There's no need to apologize," she said. "If you want to leave me, that's OK. I won't say a thing. Do you want to leave me?"

"I don't know," I replied. "Can I explain what's happened?"

"You mean about you and that woman?"

"Yes," I said.

She shook her head emphatically. "I don't want to hear anything about her. Don't make me suffer any more than I already have. I don't care what kind of relationship the two of you have or what plans you've made. I don't want to hear about it. What I do want to know is whether or not you want to leave me. I don't need the house, or money – or anything. If you want the children, take them. I'm serious. If you want to leave me, just say the word. That's all I want to know. I don't want to hear anything else. Just yes or no."

"I don't know," I said.

"You mean you don't know if you want to leave me or not?"

"No. I don't know if I'm even capable of giving you an answer."

"When will you know?"

I shook my head.

"Well, then, take your time and think about it." She sighed. "I don't mind waiting. Take as long as you like."

After that, I slept on the sofa in the living room. Sometimes the children would get up in the middle of the night and ask me why I was sleeping there. I explained that my snoring was so loud these days that their mother and I had decided to sleep in separate rooms. Otherwise Mum wouldn't get any sleep. One of the kids would snuggle up next to me on the sofa. And I would hug her tight. Sometimes I could hear Yukiko in the bedroom, crying.

For the next two weeks I spent every day endlessly reliving memories. I'd recall every single detail of the night I had spent with Shimamoto, trying to tease out some meaning. Trying to find a message. I remembered the warmth of her in my arms. Her arms sticking out of the sleeves of her white dress. The Nat King Cole songs. The fire in the stove. I called up each and every word we had spoken.

From out of those words, these of hers: *There is no middle ground with me. No middle-ground objects exist and where there are no such objects, there is no middle ground.*

And these words of mine: *I've already decided, Shimamoto-san. I thought about it when you were gone, and I made my decision.*

I remembered her eyes, looking at me in the car. That intense gaze burned into my cheeks. It was more than a mere glance. The smell of death hovered over her. She was planning to die. That's why she came to Hakone – to die, together with me.

"And I will take all of you. Do you understand that? *Do you understand what that means?*"

When she had said that, Shimamoto wanted my life. Only now did I understand.

I had come to a final conclusion and so had she. Why was I so blind? After a night of making love, she planned to grab the steering wheel of the BMW as we drove back to Tokyo and kill us both. No other options remained for her. But something stopped her. And holding everything inside, she disappeared.

What desperate dead end had she reached? Why? And, more important, who had driven her to such desperation? Why, finally, was death the only possible escape? I was grasping for clues, playing the detective, but I came up empty-handed.

She just vanished, along with her secrets. No *probablys* or *in a whiles* this time – she just slipped away silently. Our bodies had become one, yet in the end she refused to open up her heart to me.

Some kinds of thing, once they go forward, can never go back to where they began, Hajime, she would no doubt tell me. In the middle of the night, lying on my sofa, I could hear her voice spinning out these words. *As you said, how wonderful it would be if the two of us could go off somewhere and begin life again. Unfortunately, I can't get out of where I am. It's a physical impossibility.*

And then Shimamoto was a sixteen-year-old girl again, standing in front of sunflowers in a garden, smiling shyly. *I really shouldn't have gone to see you. I knew that from the beginning. I could predict that it would turn out like this. But I couldn't stand not to. I just had to see you, and when I did, I had to speak to you. Hajime – that's me. I don't plan it, but everything I touch gets ruined in the end.*

I would never see her again, except in memory. She was here and now she's gone. There is no middle ground. *Probably* is a word you may find south of the border. But never, ever, west of the sun.

Every day, I scanned the papers from top to bottom for articles about women suicides. Lots of people kill themselves, I discovered, but it was always someone else. As far as I knew, this beautiful thirty-seven-year-old woman with the loveliest of smiles was still alive. Though she was gone from me for ever.

On the surface, my days were the same as ever. I'd drive the kids back and forth to the nursery school, the three of us singing songs as we went. Sometimes in the line of cars in front of the nursery school I'd see the young woman in the 260E, and we'd talk. Talking to her made me able to forget, at least for a while. Our subjects were limited, as always. We'd exchange the latest news about the Aoyama neighbourhood, natural foods, clothes. The usual.

At work, too, I made my usual rounds. I'd put on my suit and go to the bars every night, make small talk with the regulars, listen to the opinions and complaints of the staff, remember little things like giving a birthday present to an employee. Treat any musicians who happened to drop by to dinner, check the cocktails to make sure they were up to par, make sure the piano was in tune, keep an eye out for rowdy drunks – I did it all. Any problems I straightened out in a flash. Everything ran like clockwork, but the thrill was gone. No one suspected, though. On the surface I was the same as always. Actually, I was friendlier, kinder, more talkative than ever. But as I sat on a bar stool, looking around my establishment, everything looked monotonous, lustreless. No longer a carefully crafted, colourful castle in the air, what lay before me was a typical noisy bar – artificial, superficial and shabby. A stage set, props built for the sole purpose of getting drunks to part with their cash. Any illusions to the contrary had disappeared in a puff of smoke. All because Shimamoto would never grace these places again. Never again would she sit at the bar; never again would I see her smile as she ordered a drink.

My routine at home was unchanged too. I ate dinner with the family and on Sundays took the kids for a walk or to the zoo. Yukiko, at least on the surface, treated me as she always had. We talked about all kinds of things. We were like childhood friends who happened to be living under the same roof. There were certain words we couldn't speak, certain facts we didn't acknowledge. But there was no unconcealed hostility in the air. We just didn't touch each other. At night we slept separately – I on the sofa, Yukiko in the bedroom. Outwardly, that was the only change in our lives.

Sometimes I couldn't stand the fact that we were just going through the motions, acting out our assigned roles. Something crucial to us was lost, yet still we could carry on as before. I felt awful. This kind of empty, meaningless life was hurting Yukiko deeply. I wanted to give her an answer to her question, but I couldn't. Of course I didn't want to leave her, but who was I to say that? Me – the man who had been going to throw his whole family away. Just because Shimamoto was gone, never to return, didn't mean I could blithely bounce back to the life I'd had and pretend nothing had happened. Life isn't that easy and I don't think it should be. Besides, lingering images of Shimamoto were still too clear, too real. Every time I closed my eyes, every detail of her body floated before me. My palms remembered the feel of her skin and her voice whispering in my ear wouldn't leave me. I couldn't make love to Yukiko with those images still implanted so firmly in my brain.

I wanted to be alone, so knowing nothing else I went swimming every morning at the pool. Then I'd go to my office, stare at the ceiling, and lose myself in daydreams of Shimamoto. With Yukiko's question hanging before me unanswered, I was living in a void. I couldn't go on for ever like that. It wasn't right. As a human being, as a husband, as a father, I had to live up to my responsibilities. Yet as long as these illusions surrounded me, I was paralysed. It was even worse when it rained, for then I was struck by the delusion that Shimamoto would show up: quietly opening the door, bringing with her the scent of rain. I could picture the smile on her face. When I said something wrong, she would silently shake her head, smiling all the while. My words lost their strength and, like raindrops glued to the window, slowly parted company with reality. On rainy nights I could barely breathe. The rain twisted time and reality.

When I grew exhausted with these daydreams, I stared at the scenery outside. I was abandoned in a lifeless, dried-out land. The visions had drained colour from the world. Everything, every scene before me, lay flat, mere makeshift. Every object was gritty, the colour of sand. The parting words of my old school friend haunted me. *Lots of different ways to live. And lots of different ways to die. But in the end . . . all that remains is a desert.*

The following week, as if they had been lying in wait, strange events ambushed me one after another. On Monday morning, for no special reason I recalled the envelope with one hundred thousand yen and decided to look for it. Many years before I had put it in a drawer in the desk in my office, a locked drawer, second from the top. When I moved into the office, I had put some other valuables together with the envelope in that drawer; other than occasionally checking to see that it was there, I never touched it. But now the envelope was gone. This was strange, uncanny even, for I had absolutely no memory of moving it. I was certain of that. Just to make sure, I pulled open the other drawers and checked them from top to bottom. No envelope.

I tried to remember when I'd last seen it. I couldn't pin down an exact date. It wasn't all that long ago, but not so recently, either. A month ago, maybe two. Three at the most.

Bewildered, I sat down on my chair and stared at the drawer. Maybe someone had broken into the room, unlocked the drawer and removed the envelope. That wasn't likely, though – the drawer contained more cash and valuables, which were untouched. Yet it *was* within the realms of possibility. Or maybe unconsciously I'd disposed of the envelope and for whatever reason erased the memory from my mind. OK, I told myself, what does it matter? I was going to get rid of it some day. I'd just saved myself the trouble, right?

But once I acknowledged that the envelope had disappeared, its existence and non-existence traded places in my consciousness. A strange feeling, like vertigo, took hold of me. A conviction that the envelope had never actually existed swelled up inside me, violently chipping away at my mind, crushing and greedily devouring the certainty I'd had that the envelope was *real*.

Because memory and sensations are so uncertain, so biased, we always rely on a certain reality – call it an *alternate* reality – to prove the reality of events. To what extent facts we recognize as such really *are* as they seem, and to what extent these are facts merely because we label them as such, is an impossible distinction to draw. Therefore, in order to pin down reality *as* reality, we need another reality to relativize the first. Yet that other reality requires a third reality to serve as its grounding. An endless chain is created within our consciousness, and it is the maintenance of this chain which produces the sensation that we are actually here, that we ourselves exist. But something can happen to sever that chain and we are at a loss. What is real? Is reality on this side of the break in the chain? Or over there, on the other side?

What I felt at that point, then, was this kind of cut-off sensation. I closed the drawer, deciding to forget all about it. I should have thrown that money away when I first got it. Keeping it was a mistake.

On Wednesday afternoon of the same week I was driving down Gaien Higashidori, when I spied a woman who resembled Shimamoto. She had on blue cotton trousers, a beige raincoat and white gym shoes. And she dragged one leg as she walked. As soon as I saw her, everything around me froze. A lump of air forced its way up from my chest to my throat.

Shimamoto, I thought. I drove past her to check her out in the rear mirror, but her face was hidden in the crowd. I slammed on my brakes, earning an earful of horn from the car behind me. The way the woman held herself, and the length of her hair – it was Shimamoto exactly. I wanted to stop the car at once, but all the parking spots along the road were full. Two hundred metres or so further on, I finally found a place and managed to squeeze my car in, then I ran back to find her. But she was nowhere to be seen. I ran around like a lunatic. She had a bad leg, so she couldn't have gone too far, I told myself. Shoving people aside, jaywalking across streets, I ran up the pedestrian overpass and looked down on all the passers-by below. My shirt was soaked with sweat. Soon, though, a revelation dawned on me. She had been dragging the opposite leg. *And Shimamoto's leg was no longer bad.*

I shook my head and sighed deeply. Something must be wrong with me. I felt dizzy, my strength drained away. Leaning against the pedestrian signal, I stared at my feet for a while. The light turned from green to red, from red to green again. People crossed the street, waited, crossed, with me immobile, collapsed against the post, gasping for breath.

Suddenly I looked up and saw Izumi's face. She was in a taxi which had stopped right in front of me. From the side window she was staring right at me. The taxi had halted at the red light and, at most, three feet separated her face and mine. She was no longer the seventeen-year-old girl I used to know, but I recognized her at once. The girl I'd held in my arms twenty years before, the first girl I kissed. The girl who, on that autumn afternoon so long ago, took off her clothes and lost her suspender. People might change over twenty years, but I knew this was her. *Children are afraid of her,* my old friend had said. When I'd heard that, I didn't understand what he meant. I couldn't grasp what those words were attempting to convey. But now, with Izumi right before my eyes, I understood. Her face had nothing you could call an expression. No, that's not an entirely accurate way of putting it. I should put it this way: like a room from which every last stick of furniture had been taken, anything you could possibly call an expression had been removed, leaving nothing behind. Not a trace of feeling grazed her face; it was like the bottom of a deep ocean, silent and dead. And with that utterly expressionless face, she was staring at me. At least I think she was looking at me. Her eyes were gazing straight ahead in my direction, yet her face showed me nothing. Or rather, what it showed was this: an infinite blank.

I stood there dumbfounded, speechless. Barely able to support my body, I breathed slowly. For a moment or two my sense of self broke down, its very outlines melting away into a thick, syrupy mess. Unconsciously I reached out my hand and touched the window of the cab, stroked the surface of the glass with my fingertips. I had no idea why. A couple of passers-by, startled, stopped and stared. But I couldn't help myself. Through the glass, I slowly stroked that face-less face. Izumi didn't move a muscle or so much as blink. Was she dead? No, not dead. She was still alive, in an unblinking world. In a deep, silent world behind that pane of glass, she lived. And her lips, motionless, spoke of an infinite nothingness.

The light finally changed to green, and the taxi moved off. Izumi's face was unchanged to the end. I stood rooted to the spot, watching until the taxi was swallowed up in the surge of cars.

I walked back to my car and slumped into the seat. I had to get out of there. As I was about to turn on the engine I was hit by a sudden wave of nausea, as if I was going to spew my guts out. But I didn't vomit. Resting both hands on the steering wheel, I sat there for a good fifteen minutes. My underarms were drenched in sweat, and an awful smell rose from my body. This wasn't the body that Shimamoto had loved so gently. It was the body of a middle-aged man, giving off an acrid stench.

A few minutes later, a policeman came up to my car and knocked on the window. I rolled it down. "You can't park here, sir," he said, looking around inside. "Move your car away from here." I nodded and started the motor.

"You look terrible. Do you feel sick?" the policeman asked me.

Wordlessly, I shook my head. And started driving.

It took me several hours to recover. I was drained, completely, leaving an empty shell behind. A hollow sound reverberated through my body. I parked my car inside Aoyama Cemetery and stared listlessly through the windscreen at the sky beyond. Izumi was waiting for me there. She was always somewhere, waiting for me. On some street corner, beyond some pane of glass, waiting for me to appear. Watching me. I just hadn't noticed.

For several days afterwards, I couldn't speak. I'd open my mouth to talk, but the words would disappear, as if the utter nothingness that was Izumi had taken over.

After that strange encounter, though, the after images of Shimamoto began, gradually, to fade. Colour returned to the world and I no longer had the helpless feeling that I was walking on the surface of the moon. Vaguely, as if looking through a glass window at changes happening to someone else, I could detect a minute shift in gravity and a gradual sloughing off of something that had clung to me.

Something inside me was severed and disappeared. Silently. For ever.

While the trio were on their break, I went up to the pianist and told him he no longer needed to play "Star-Crossed Lovers". I mustered up the friendliest smile I could. "You've played it for me enough. It's about time to stop."

He looked at me, as if weighing something in his mind. The two of us were friends, had shared a few drinks and gone beyond the usual polite conversation.

"I don't quite understand," he said. "You don't want me to go out of my way to play that song? Or you don't want me ever to play that song again? There's a big difference, and I'd like to be clear about this."

"I don't want you to play it," I said.

"You don't like the way I play it?"

"I have no problems with your playing. It's great. There aren't many people who can handle that tune the way you do."

"So it's the tune itself you don't want to hear any more?"

"You could say that," I replied.

"Sounds a little like *Casablanca* to me!" he said.

"I suppose so," I said.

Since then, sometimes when he catches sight of me, the pianist breaks into a few bars of "As Time Goes By".

The reason I didn't want to hear that tune again had nothing to do with memories of Shimamoto. *The song just didn't do to me what it used to.* Why, I can't say. The special something I'd found ages ago in that melody was no longer there. It was still a beautiful tune, but nothing more. And I had no intention of lingering over the corpse of a beautiful song.

"What are you thinking about?" Yukiko asked me as she came into the room.

It was two-thirty in the morning. I was lying on the sofa, staring at the ceiling.

"I was thinking about a desert," I said.

"A desert?" she asked. She'd sat down next to my feet and was looking at me. "What kind of desert?"

"Just a regular desert. With sand dunes and a few cacti. Lots of things are there, living there."

"Am I included in this desert too?" she asked.

"Of course you are," I said. "All of us are living there. But actually what's really living is the desert itself. Like it is in the film."

"What film?"

"The Disney film *The Living Desert*. A documentary about the desert. Didn't you see it when you were little?"

"No," she said. I thought that was a bit strange. Everybody in my elementary school had been herded off to the cinema to watch it. But Yukiko was five years younger than me. She might have been too young to see it when it came out.

"Why don't we rent it next Sunday and watch it together? It's a good film. The scenery's beautiful and there're all sorts of animals and flowers. The kids will like it."

Yukiko smiled at me. It had been such a long time since I'd seen her smile.

"Do you want to leave me?" she asked.

"Yukiko, I love you," I said.

"Maybe you do, but I'm asking you whether you want to leave me. The answer is either yes or no. I won't accept any other."

"I don't want to leave you," I said. I shook my head. "I probably don't have the right to say this, but I don't want to leave you. If I left you now, I don't know what would happen to me. I don't want to be lonely ever again. I'd rather die."

She stretched out a hand and placed it on my chest. And

181

looked deep into my eyes. "Forget about rights. I don't think anyone has those kinds of rights," she said.

Feeling the warmth of her hand on my chest, I thought of death. I might well have died on that day on the highway with Shimamoto. If I had, my body would not exist. I would be gone, lost for ever. Like so many other things. But here I am. And here is Yukiko's warm hand on my chest.

"Yukiko," I said, "I love you very much. I loved you from the first day I met you and I still feel the same. If I hadn't met you, my life would have been unbearable. For that I am grateful beyond words. Yet here I am, hurting you. Because I'm a selfish, hopeless, worthless human being. For no apparent reason, I hurt the people around me and end up hurting myself. Ruining someone else's life and my own. Not because I want to. But that's how it ends up."

"No argument there," Yukiko said quietly. Traces of her smile remained at the corners of her mouth. "You are definitely a selfish, hopeless person and, yes, you have hurt me."

I looked at her for a while. Nothing in her words seemed to blame me. She was neither angry nor sad. She was merely explaining the obvious.

I took my time, trying to find the right words. "I always feel as if I'm struggling to become someone else. As if I'm trying to find a new place, grab hold of a new life, a new personality. I suppose it's part of growing up, yet it's also an attempt to re-invent myself. By becoming a different me, I could free myself of everything. I seriously believed I could escape myself – as long as I made the effort. But I always hit a dead end. No matter where I go, I still end up me. What's missing never changes. The scenery may change, but I'm still the same old incomplete person. The same missing elements torture me with a hunger that I can never satisfy. I think that lack itself is as close as I'll come to defining myself. For your

182

sake, I'd like to become a new person. It may not be easy, but if I give it my all, perhaps I *can* manage to change. The truth is, though, if I were put back in the same situation, I might well do the same thing all over again. I might very well hurt you all over again. I can't promise anything. That's what I meant when I said I had no right. I just don't have the confidence to win over that force in me."

"And you've always been trying to escape that force?"

"I think so," I said.

Her hand still rested on my chest. "You poor man," she said. As if she were reading aloud something written large on a wall. Maybe it really was written on the wall, I thought.

"I don't know what to say," I said. "I know I don't want to leave you. But I don't know if that's the correct answer. I don't even know if that's something I myself can choose. Yukiko, you're suffering. I can see that. I can feel your hand here. But there's something beyond what can be seen or felt. Call it feelings. Or possibilities. These well up from somewhere and are mixed together inside me. They're not something I can choose or can give an answer to."

Yukiko was silent for a long time. Every so often, a truck rolled by outside. I looked out of the window but could see nothing. Just the unnamed time and space linking night and dawn.

"The last few weeks, I really did think I would die," Yukiko said. "I'm not saying this to threaten you. It's a fact. That's how lonely and sad I was. Dying is not that hard. Like the air being sucked slowly out of a room, the will to live was slowly seeping out of me. When you feel like that, dying doesn't seem like such a big deal. I never even thought of the children. What would happen to them after I died didn't enter my mind. That's how lonely I felt. You didn't know that, did you? You have never seriously given it any thought, have you? What I was feeling, what I was thinking, what I might do."

I didn't say anything. She took her hand away from my chest and laid it in her lap.

"Anyhow, the reason I didn't die, the reason I'm still alive, is that I thought if you were to come back to me, I would be able to take you back. It's not a question of rights, or right or wrong. Maybe you are a hopeless person. A worthless person. And you might very well hurt me again. But that's not what's important here. You don't understand a thing."

"Most likely I don't," I said.

"And you don't ask anything," she said.

I opened my mouth to say something, but the words wouldn't come out. She was right: I never did ask her anything. Why didn't I? I had no idea.

"Rights are what you build from now on," Yukiko said. "Or rather, *we* build. We thought we'd constructed a lot together, but actually we hadn't made a thing. Life went too smoothly. We were too happy. Don't you think so?"

I nodded.

Yukiko folded her arms over her chest and looked at me. "I used to have dreams too, you know. But somewhere along the line they disappeared. Before I met you. I killed them. I crushed them and threw them away. Like some internal organ you no longer need and you rip out of your body. I don't know whether that was the right thing to do. But it was the only thing I could do at the time . . . Sometimes I have this dream. The same dream over and over again. Someone is carrying something in both hands, and comes up to me and says, 'Here, you've forgotten something.' I've been very happy living with you. I've wanted for nothing and never had any complaints. Still, something is chasing me. I wake up in the middle of the night, covered in sweat. I'm being chased by what I threw away. You think you're the only one being chased, but you're wrong. You're not the only one who's thrown away something, who's lost something. Do you understand what I'm saying?"

"I think so," I said.

"Maybe you will hurt me again. I don't know how I'll react then. Or maybe next time I'll hurt you. No one can promise anything. Neither of us can make any promises. But I do still love you."

I held her and stroked her hair.

"Yukiko," I said, "tomorrow let's begin again. It's too late today. I want to start out the right way, with a brand-new day."

Yukiko looked at me for a while. "I think that you still haven't asked me anything."

"I'd like to start a new life beginning tomorrow. What do you think?" I asked.

"I think that's a good idea," she said, a faint smile on her lips.

After Yukiko went back to the bedroom, I lay for a while on the sofa, staring at the ceiling. It was an ordinary apartment ceiling, nothing special. But still I stared at it closely. Every once in a while, a car's headlights would shine on it. I had no more illusions. The feel of Shimamoto's breasts, her voice, the scent of her skin – all had faded. Izumi's expressionless face floated across my mind. And the feel of the taxi's window separating us. I closed my eyes and thought of Yukiko. Again and again I thought over what she had said. Eyes closed, I listened to the movements within my body. I might very well be changing. And I had to change.

I don't know if I have the strength to care for Yukiko and the children, I thought. No more visions can help me, weaving special dreams just for me. As far as the eye can see, the void is simply that – a void. I've been in that void before and forced myself to adjust. And now, finally, I end up where I began and I'd better get used to it. No one will weave dreams for me – it is my turn to weave dreams for others. That's what I have to do. Such dreams may have no power, but if my own life is to have any meaning at all, that is what I have to do.

Probably.

As the dawn approached, I gave up trying to sleep. I threw a cardigan over my pyjamas, padded out to the kitchen, and made some coffee. I sat at the kitchen table and watched the sky grow lighter by the minute. It had been a long time since I'd seen the dawn. At one end of the sky a line of blue appeared, and like blue ink on a piece of paper it spread slowly across the horizon. If you gathered together all the shades of blue in the world and picked the bluest, the epitome of blue, this was the colour you would choose. I rested my elbows on the table and looked at that scene, my mind blank. When the sun showed itself over the horizon, that blue was swallowed up by ordinary sunlight. A single cloud floated above the cemetery, a pure white cloud, its edges distinct. A cloud so sharply etched you could write on it. A new day had begun. But what this day would bring, I had no idea.

I would take my daughters to nursery school and go swimming. The same as always. I remembered the pool I used to swim in during junior high. The smell of the place, the way voices echoed off the ceiling. I was in the midst of becoming something new. Standing in front of the mirror, I could see the changes in my body. At night, in the stillness, I swore I could hear the sound of my flesh growing. I was about to be clothed in a new self, about to step into a place where I'd never been.

Sitting at the kitchen table, I watched the single cloud over the cemetery. The cloud didn't move an inch. It was stationary, nailed to the spot. Time to wake my daughters. It was well past dawn, and they had to get up. They were the ones who needed this new day, much more than I ever would. I'd go to their bedroom, pull back the covers, rest my hand on their warm bodies and announce the beginning of a new day. That's what I had to do. But somehow I couldn't stand up from the kitchen table. All strength was drained from my body, as if someone had crept up behind me and silently pulled the plug. Both elbows on the table, I covered my face with my palms.

Inside that darkness, I saw rain falling on the sea. Rain softly falling on a vast sea, with no one there to see it. The rain strikes the surface of the sea, yet even the fish don't know it is raining.

Until someone came and rested a hand lightly on my shoulder, my thoughts were of the sea.

Haruki Murakami

AFTER THE QUAKE

'How does Murakami manage to make poetry while writing of contemporary life and emotions? I am weak-kneed with admiration'
Independent on Sunday

'Even in the slipperiest of Mr Murakami's stories, pinpoints of detail flash out warm with life'
New York Times

The economy was booming. People had more money than they knew what to do with. And then the earthquake struck. For the characters in *after the quake*, the Kobe earthquake is an echo from a past they buried long ago. Satsuki has a spent thirty years hating one man: a lover who destroyed her chances of having children. Did her desire for revenge cause the earthquake? Junpei's estranged parents live in Kobe. Should he contact them? Miyake left his family in Kobe to make midnight bonfires on a beach hundreds of miles away. Four-year-old Sala has nightmares that the Earthquake Man is trying to stuff her inside a little box. Katagiri returns home to find a giant frog in his apartment on a mission to save Tokyo from a massive burrowing worm. 'When he gets angry, he causes earthquakes,' says Frog. 'And right now he is very, very angry.'

'Murakami is one of the best writers around'
Time Out

VINTAGE

BY HARUKI MURAKAMI
ALSO AVAILABLE FROM VINTAGE

☐	after the quake	0099448564	£6.99
☐	Dance Dance Dance	0099448769	£7.99
☐	The Elephant Vanishes	0099448750	£7.99
☐	Hard-boiled Wonderland and the End of the World	0099448785	£7.99
☐	Norwegian Wood	0099448823	£7.99
☐	Sputnik Sweetheart	0099448475	£6.99
☐	Underground	0099461099	£7.99
☐	A Wild Sheep Chase	0099448777	£7.99
☐	The Wind-up Bird Chronicle	0099448793	£7.99
☐	Kafka on the Shore	0099458322	£7.99
☐	Birthday Stories	0099481553	£7.99